What the critics are saying...

"Private Games is like an evening with your best friends – a hell lot of fun, full of surprises and laugh-out-loud-moments." ~ *Frauke, Mon-Boudoir*

"...three extremely hot, arousing, and sexually challenging stories that had me reaching for the ice." ~ *Anne, Enchanted in Romance*

"...exhilarating and hilarious." ~ *Jennifer Brooks, Coffee Time Romance*

Tawny Taylor

An Ellora's Cave Romantica Publication

www.ellorascave.com

Private Games

ISBN # 1419952196

Edited by: Martha Punches
Cover art by: Syneca

Electronic book Publication: October, 2004
Trade paperback Publication: July, 2005

Warning:

The following material contains graphic sexual content meant for mature readers. *Private Games* has been rated *E-rotic* by a minimum of three independent reviewers.

Ellora's Cave Publishing offers three levels of Romantica™ reading entertainment: S (S-ensuous), E (E-rotic), and X (X-treme).

S-e*nsuous* love scenes are explicit and leave nothing to the imagination.

E-*rotic* love scenes are explicit, leave nothing to the imagination, and are high in volume per the overall word count. In addition, some E-rated titles might contain fantasy material that some readers find objectionable, such as bondage, submission, same sex encounters, forced seductions, etc. E-rated titles are the most graphic titles we carry; it is common, for instance, for an author to use words such as "fucking", "cock", "pussy", etc., within their work of literature.

X-*treme* titles differ from E-rated titles only in plot premise and storyline execution. Unlike E-rated titles, stories designated with the letter X tend to contain controversial subject matter not for the faint of heart.

Also by Tawny Taylor:

Lessons in Lust Major

Passion In A Pear Tree

Tempting Fate

Wet and Wilde

Contents

Playing for Keeps
~11~

Master, May I?
~85~

A Game of Risk
~171~

Trademarks Acknowledgement

The author acknowledges the trademarked status and trademark owners of the following wordmarks mentioned in this work of fiction:

Victoria's Secret: V Secret Catalogue, Inc.
Outback Steakhouse: OS Asset, Inc.
UPS: United Parcel Service of America, Inc.
Dewalt: Black & Decker Corporation
Mustang: Ford Motor Company
Mack Truck: Mack Trucks, Inc.
Risk: Hasbro, Inc.

Playing For Keeps

Chapter One

Sure, that's all Detroit needs: three lunatic women running around in clothing that could barely be legal and putting themselves in asinine situations…so why am I even considering playing along?

Maddy Beaudet gave her two closest friends, Candace and Nic, an intimidating stare, or so she hoped. But the resulting laughter pealing through her living room suggested she'd failed. Miserably. Not that she was surprised. Her visage was never one most people would call intimidating.

"Oh, come on, party-pooper." Candace drained her glass and set it on the coffee table before reaching for the wine bottle. "You said it yourself. You need a change."

Maddy snatched the bottle away before her well-meaning but half-cocked friend refilled her glass again. In the process, she knocked her cat from his favorite spot, curled up on her lap. She reached for him, but he snubbed her. "Sorry, Jack, but one more dose and that woman would be near impossible to reason with." Knowing it took him an hour, maybe two, to quit sulking—the animal was no better than a man—she turned to her friends. "Yeah, a change. As in a new job. Maybe some new clothes. Nothing major…like this!"

"It isn't major. It's a simple game among friends, for crying out loud. Now, give me that bottle."

"No way. And the game you're suggesting isn't just your run of the mill game. It's a man-chasing contest." She lifted her hand, holding the bottle out of Candace's reach. "That's…that's…"

"A hell of a lot of fun! Is there any other kind of game?" Nic said behind her, right before she filched the bottle from Maddy and handed it to Candace.

"Word games. Board games. Football games." Maddy groaned as she watched Candace grin and drain the remaining wine from the bottle. "You have no idea what you're doing."

Nic nodded. "Oh, yes I do."

"What women, graduated from elementary school, participate in such ridiculous contests?"

"Lots of them. It's the latest craze. It was even on *Oprah*. I got this on the Internet. It's the number one seller on all the major online retailers." Candace stood up and shook and gyrated like she did on a nightclub dance floor. Her gold hair whipped around like an enraged mop, if there was such a thing. "Relax, you need to shake things up a bit."

"Yeah, shake things up," Nic echoed.

Maddy swallowed a chuckle at Candace and poked her index finger at Nic. "I don't need any more help from you."

"Oh, yes you do."

She scowled at her traitorous friend before turning back to the hyperactive woman in front of her.

Candace looked like she was preparing to run a marathon. Hopping up and down, she half-sung, "You have no idea what might happen."

"If I jump up and down like that, I might bust loose from this bra."

"We better put this away for safekeeping until we get back." Candace gathered the game board and pieces, tossed them in the box and then shoved the deck of Challenge cards in her purse. Then she reached down and gripped Maddy's hands. "Worse things could happen. By the way, that bra does nothing for you."

"Yeah. Like I could lose my two thousand bucks."

"We all put in the same money. That was the deal. Just think about it. You could win! The trip of a lifetime. You've got a thirty-percent chance." With a yank Candace pulled Maddy to her feet and headed toward the door. "Let's go."

"Go where?"

"Shopping first. And then you pull your first Challenge card, and we're going along to make sure you go through with it."

Maddy dragged her feet as she half-walked, half-slunk onto the porch. "How thoughtful."

"It's my pleasure." Candace slammed the door behind them as they headed out to her car and then pushed Maddy toward the passenger side. "Someday you'll thank me."

"I doubt that."

"I don't. Hey, Nic, you'd better drive. That last glass of wine hit me pretty hard."

Nic drove to the mall at her usual breakneck speed. It was a wonder Candace's car sat flat on four wheels at traffic lights since most of the time it felt as though it teetered on two. By all rights, there shouldn't be any rubber remaining on the right tires.

And it was a wonder Maddy arrived at their destination with the contents of her stomach still neatly packed away where they belonged.

On wobbly legs, she followed her devious but beloved friends into the building and faithfully tried on every outfit, no matter how obscene she thought they were. Eventually, she settled for a simple but sexy black dress and moderate heels. As she fastened the sparkly choker around her neck, she had to admit, the outfit made her feel a little naughty. A little sexy and brave. Maybe the game wouldn't be so bad.

And the prize was definitely something to think about. A whole week in the Caribbean! The recipient of a modest administrator's salary, she'd never dreamed of taking a trip like that. The closest she'd figured she'd ever get was watching that yummy pirate movie with Johnny Depp. Jack Sparrow...she sighed.

What if she did win? Oh...wouldn't that be something?

Waiting for Candace and Nic to change into their chosen outfits, she let her eyelids drop closed for just a moment and tried to imagine what a trip to tropical sandy beaches would be like.

Did they really have sexy cabana boys at those resorts? And massages? And crystal-clear ocean waters? And men in tiny swimming briefs with glittering water droplets clinging to their chests…mmm…?

Too bad there weren't pirates anymore.

Unless maybe they had pirate shows.

And there would be no bosses screaming in her face for a whole week… Oh… She had to win! She felt herself smiling.

"What's this?" she heard Candace say.

She opened her eyes.

Candace grinned. "Do I see the beginnings of a change of heart? Hmmm?"

Taking in the sight of one barely clad blonde-haired, blue-eyed bombshell and a similarly dressed Nic with deep auburn hair and green eyes, Maddy tried to suppress the smile still pulling at her cheeks. "Me? Nope. I still think the game's stupid. But," she sighed, "I intend to win, stupid or not."

"Now, that's the right attitude! Kinda. Good for you." Nic gave her a friendly tap on the shoulder. "And dressed like that, I think you just might win."

Candace looked from Nic to Maddy and back again as they stood at the cash register. "Now, let's make this a fair and friendly competition, girls, okay? We don't have an independent judge, so no cheating."

"Of course." Nic nodded, handing the clerk her credit card.

"Sure." The minute Maddy uttered her answer, she was snagged by the arms and led, teetering on her heels, and taking baby steps because her clinging dress left little room for long strides, to the parking lot. Once in the car, she watched Candace hand the deck of cards to Nic who shuffled them and handed them back.

"Okay, draw one." Candace held the cards in her palm.

"Does it have to be the top one?" Maddy asked, hesitating after seeing the look the two friends passed each other with the cards. *No cheating, my butt!*

Candace scowled. "What? You don't trust us?"

"Nope."

"Well!" Candace made a good show of looking insulted, but when Maddy didn't back down, she muttered, "No, it doesn't have to be the top one."

Maddy picked her card, from somewhere toward the bottom of the pile and attempted to read it, but before she'd gotten past the first word, "Go", Nic plucked it out of her hand and read it aloud.

"Go to the hottest club in your city and collect the name and phone number of the hottest man in the room."

"Well, that one isn't so bad," Candace murmured.

Maddy breathed a sigh of relief. Having scanned a few of those cards back at her place before they'd left, she knew what crazy stunts were written on a few of them. And if she were a betting woman, she'd put money on the fact that one of the worst sat smack-dab on the top of the stack. "It's bad enough. Let's go get this over with. I'm tired, and I have *Pirates of the Caribbean* for one more night."

"Why don't you just buy the stupid movie? You've watched the damn thing at least three times already."

"You know what? I just might." She fastened her seat belt and braced herself for the ride ahead.

Thankfully, the drive to the hottest nightclub, by most standards, in the tri-county area was a short one. And so, after a brief but hair-raising ride, Maddy staggered from the car to the entry, squinting against the late summer's sun glaring from the west. She begrudgingly paid the atrocious cover, and fell instantly blind in the dim interior. "We got here a little early, don'tcha' think?" she asked, feeling her way down a narrow hallway and blinking to try to accustom her eyes to the darkness. "The place is bound to be empty. No one comes to bars before ten." Her hand ran across something soft, and she realized suddenly that she'd just felt up someone standing against the wall.

And that lump could only be one thing!

Out of reflex, she jerked her hand back. "Omigod! I'm so sorry."

"I'm not," a warm voice that felt like velvet sliding over her body responded.

Now, more irritated than ever at her maladjusted eyes, she blinked again and concentrated on focusing, realizing after a few bloated moments she was staring at a black-clothed chest. Very wide.

She tipped her head to look up, and up, and up. Good God, the guy had to be nearly seven feet tall. Then she caught sight of his face, and even in the shadows, she could tell he was breathtaking.

He smiled.

She quit breathing.

"Hello there," he drawled, slow and delicious, making each sound smooth and silky, and she fought to keep herself vertical. If there ever was such a thing as a fuck-me voice, this hunk had one.

And he had the fuck-me look down pat, too.

"Hi," she squeaked. Then she jumped when something, or someone, poked her in the ass. She turned her head.

Candace and Nic. Couldn't they just disappear?

Candace stepped forward, staring over Maddy's head at Mr. Tall, Dark and Dangerous. "Hi, there. I'm Candace. Looks like my friend's lost her tongue..."

Yeah, it fell on the floor...

"...her name is Maddy."

"Is that short for Madeline?" he asked, his gaze still riveted to Maddy's face, which she felt heating.

Lifting cool fingers to chill her flaming cheeks, she hoped he couldn't tell in the dim light exactly how bad she was blushing. "Yes. Madeline Beaudet, but no one calls me that. At least not since grade school. I've always preferred Maddy," she heard herself ramble.

He reached out and gently toyed with the hand resting on her face. His thick fingers tickled its back, the clefts between her fingers, her wrist. It was the most erotic, sensual touch she'd ever experienced from a complete stranger. And it left her feeling like gelatin forgotten outside on a hot summer day. "Your name is very sexy. French?"

"Um..." *French what? French wine? French kiss? Sure!*

"Are you French?" He smiled, letting those teasing, wandering fingers travel up her arm and tug on the very thin, very fragile strap holding her dress up at the shoulder.

What a disaster it would be for that strap to break!

"Um... Yeah. Sorta. My family's French-Canadian."

"How interesting." He pulled on the strap, and she sighed as she felt the weight of her breast being lifted by the dress's sewn-in shelf bra. Her nipple hardened, straining against the slick, clingy material. "And speaking of interesting, I find the inhabitant of this dress absolutely fascinating."

Certain she was about to crumple like warm feta cheese, she locked her knees and prepared herself for the touch she hoped was coming. Just one touch. On her breast. A soft circle over her nipple.

He dropped the strap and her breast settled in its place next to the other one. "I suppose I've held you beautiful women up long enough."

Oh, he wasn't ditching her, was he? "No! Oh, not at all."

He smiled. "Glad to hear you don't think so. But your friends are looking a little impatient."

To hell with them! "They always look like that." She turned around, and caught a funny look from Candace. "I don't know why they'd be impatient. We're here to—" She stopped herself before she finished that sentence, recalling exactly why they were there and suddenly painfully aware of exactly why her friends were glaring at her. "Oh, God! How stupid of me. What's your name?"

"I was wondering if you were ever going to ask." He offered his hand. "Jace Michael."

"Jace," she repeated. "That's a very unusual name. And your last name is Michael?"

"It is."

"It's very nice. Is it Greek?"

"Sure is."

She spun around and caught her friends' approving glances before returning her full attention to the towering man commanding it. "Would you care for a drink?"

"That's supposed to be my line."

"Oh." She chuckled. "Sure, it is. And yes, I'd love one." She coughed, her throat dust-dry.

He reached forward and clasped her hand in his warm, large one. His skin was soft, his grip firm. His thumb tickled the back of her hand. "Follow me, Madeline," he purred.

Sure! Anywhere.

He stepped out from his hiding spot and only when he walked into the lighter bar area of the club did she realize not only how massive he was, but also how absolutely striking his features were.

If Greek gods had ever truly trod upon the earth, he was one of them. Absolutely perfect, from the top of his head down. Oh, no…not a Greek god. A pirate. Yes, that's what he reminded her of. His hair was dark and wavy, longer than the average guy might wear, but perfect for him. His eyes were dark, too. And riveting. His cheekbones high, his nose long and straight. And his mouth…*sigh*…she could just imagine what those gorgeous lips might do when they weren't busy forming that wicked smile she was seeing at the moment.

"Well, what'll it be?" he asked, breaking her train of thought.

A long, luscious kiss would be good. "Just a diet." She glanced around, suddenly curious where her friends had gone. They were nowhere in sight. She'd been deserted. "Just a diet."

"Are you sure?"

"Yeah. I need my wits about me tonight." *And speaking of deserting…I think my brain has deserted me too.*

He ordered from the bartender and handed her a glass. "Oh, really? Why's that?"

Why had they deserted her? Oh. She hadn't said that. "Why what?"

"Why do you need your wits about you tonight? Is there something special happening?"

There was that wicked grin again! She glanced down at her glass, sure the liquid was evaporating, thanks to the heat coming off Mr. Stunning. No, the glass was still full. What a surprise! She took a sip. It was still cold, too. "Special? Sure. I'm talking to you, naturally."

"Naturally." He rested a hand on the small of her back, and she felt herself lean back a fraction of an inch. Sweet Jesus, that little innocent touch felt good!

"Shall we get a table?" he whispered into her ear.

Nerve endings along her neck tap-danced with glee. *Or skip that and go straight for a hotel room? Sheesh! What are you thinking? Common sense, where have you gone?* "Sure. That would be nice." She followed his gentle lead, his hand softly propelling her forward with a firm and steady pressure.

"This way. There's a private table in the corner." He pointed toward a dark spot to the left.

She squinted, trying to make out the table in the shadows. "I take it you've been here a few times. I'd never know there was anything back in that corner." Then she glanced around the notably empty club. Heck, they could sit in the room's dead center and still have privacy. But for some reason, spending some quality time in a dark corner with Mr. Greek-God-Slash-Pirate left her smiling.

"Been here once before. What about you?"

"No. Never. To tell you the truth, I'm not much for the bar scene."

"I don't expect you to believe me, but neither am I." He pulled out a chair for her and waited for her to sit before he took his seat. He looked so in command, so comfortable with his surroundings, while she felt so awkward. Still, a part of her believed him.

She struggled to find something to say, partly because she found herself staring straight into his eyes. And those eyes were forever deep and dark. And partly because she was achingly aware of his knee as it brushed against hers under the table every few moments. "I believe you."

"So, what brings you here tonight?"

Fate? Gods who felt inclined to bless me? "My pesky friends. And you?"

"I'm meeting someone."

She felt her face instantly heat. "Oh…"

He chuckled, and she thought she'd die of embarrassment. She hadn't meant to be so transparent. She took another drink, wishing she'd ordered something much, much stronger. Like tequila. Why didn't she drink again?

"No, not like that. It's a business associate."

"Oh. Sure. Of course." She forced a smile and squirmed in her chair. God, this was torture! *Waiter!* She couldn't do much worse half-conscious. "So, what sort of business are you in?"

"Sales and marketing. My partner and I run a sales management firm here in Troy."

"What a coincidence. I work in a sales management office. What sort of sales?"

"We're in the golf industry."

Her eyebrows rose to the top of her face. She could feel her forehead scrunching up. "Really? Another coincidence."

"You, too?" He smiled, and she felt all warm and soupy inside. "Well, isn't it a small world. What products does your company handle?"

"Fleece and resort wear. The owners—I've only met one of them. I don't know who the other guy is. He's kind of an office mystery. This is silly, but whenever I read something with his signature, I try to make it out. But all I can get is his last name starts with an M, which makes sense since the company's name is RM Industries, and I work for Mr. Richards. Mr. M lives in California somewhere." She caught his intent look and warm-but-somewhat-empty smile and realized she was blabbering. "Anyway, the two partners manage the sales force for a company out of Utah. They sell the clothing to country clubs across the country."

His face went blank. The stunning, heart-melting smile disappeared. "You work for RM Industries?"

"Yes!" Her heart sunk as her slow-to-compute gray matter finally registered his expression. *Oh, shit! What did I say? Did I do something wrong?* "Why? Why are you looking at me like that? Do you work for a competitor?"

"Not exactly."

"Then what is it?"

Chapter Two

"There you are."

Stan. Not now! Damn it, Jace's partner had the worst timing.

Jace watched Maddy spin her head at the sound, and didn't miss the look of instant recognition that spread over her gorgeous features.

She gasped. "Mr. Richards?"

Mr. Richards. She called him mister. That fact washed away all doubt, not that there'd been much to begin with.

But what did surprise Jace was Stan's gaping mouth and up-around-the-rafters eyebrows. On a man who normally showed absolutely no emotion—the guy had the best poker face this side of the Rockies—that was something. What the hell was going on?

"Well, Ms. Beaudet, I hadn't expected to see you..." Stan's gaze wandered from her face down her barely covered chest and then back up again. He visibly swallowed, and Jace swallowed, too. Any man who beheld those tits had to. Not that he was happy about his partner's reaction to them. It almost made him want to throw the tablecloth over her. Those beauties were for his eyes only.

"I met Mr. Michael out in the lobby," she stammered.

Mr. Michael! That's my father. "Jace," he corrected.

She gave him a weak smile. "Yes. Jace."

He held back a sigh. Coming from her mouth, his name sounded so...seductive. Like a moan, a whisper, a promise.

"We were just getting acquainted. But I'm afraid I have to go now. My friends."

No! Shit! Shit! Shit! Don't leave yet. We haven't gotten properly acquainted...yet. I was looking forward to meeting your two...uh, friends... The ones that are cozy in the front of that dress of yours.

She stood and thrust her hand at him. "It was good to meet you."

He stood, took her hand, and held on for life. "Yes. You, too."

"Well," she said, smiling and obviously tugging at her imprisoned appendage. "At least now I can put a face to that scribbly signature on my checks." Her gaze met his, and currents of electricity buzzed through his body. His cock grew hard and his balls tightened.

He hadn't had that kind of reaction to a woman in ages. Why did she have to be his employee?

Knowing he had to let her go, he released her hand and watched as she turned and sashayed away. The second-skin of a dress she was wearing emphasized every drool-producing movement to perfection. He reached for his glass and gripped it tight in his fist. Tempted to either dump its contents down his throat or hurl it in frustration.

Damn it all! Here, he'd traveled across the country not to run away from an ugly, complicated situation, but more to distance himself from it, and he danced smack-dab into another one!

If he could, he'd kick his own ass.

What were the odds? Slim-to-none? How was it that he moved to the opposite side of the country and the first woman he even considered for a fling is one of his employees? *So much for no-strings sex*!

He watched her walk away, her delicious curvy ass hugged by a black velvet number that gave him an occasional glimpse of the lace band at the top of her thigh-highs. "Does she really work for us? Tell me you were lying," he murmured, knowing full well what the answer was.

"She's a sales administrator. One of the best," Stan answered. "Though I'd never have recognized her if I hadn't seen her up close. She never dresses like that. It's strictly long skirts and baggy tops for that woman, even in the summer."

"Now, that is a crime." Wishing the dark-haired goddess was sitting next to him instead of his balding business partner, he sank into his chair and swallowed the rest of his brandy before flagging the waitress. "Don't worry. I'll keep it strictly professional. I don't need the hassle of an office affair," he said more for his own benefit than Stan's.

"Good idea. I'd hate to see her work go to hell because she's too busy chasing your ass around. We need her. The samples for the spring line'll be here in a week or two, and then we'll both be hitting the road. She's gotta keep things running smooth while we're gone."

"You trust her to do all that?"

"Yep. Maddy's a hard worker. It would take three people to replace her. If you ask me, she's underemployed. A college grad, smarter than I am, works for peanuts. But hell, who am I to complain?"

Jace nodded, still trying to force the lingering memory of her gorgeous face and luscious curves from his mind. Damn, she'd had the most provocative eyes. Dark brown, almost black. And her lips. Shit, those lips! They were full, like a movie starlet's. He'd bet his balls she didn't buy those from a plastic surgeon, or those tits, either. Heavy, round, begging for his touch.

That slinky dress had left her delectable cleavage out there for the world to see. And what a sight it had been! He could imagine himself kneading that soft flesh, pushing them together and cushioning his cock in their fullness.

His hard-on tugged at his trousers, and he grimaced, shifting in his chair. It had been a long, long time since his last fuck, and his balls were screaming for relief. All he needed was a casual friend, someone who would fuck him from time to time. No strings. No commitments.

He'd thought he'd found someone. Before Stan had dropped the bomb.

"You all right, buddy?"

"Yep. Fine."

"How's that for coincidence? You didn't know who she was?"

"I figured it out right before you showed up."

Stan nodded, still staring in the general direction she'd walked. "She sure cleans up nice."

"Yeah."

"It's good to see you looking at women again. After that ugly divorce, I figured you'd write them off for good."

"Hey, I got divorced, not castrated."

"Oh, well. There are lots of other fish in the sea. How was your trip?"

"Long."

"You made the right decision. We can work together better if we live in the same state. Michigan's the best market, outside of the east coast, and Dunnert has that covered."

"Yeah. Hate the weather here, though."

"At least we don't have earthquakes."

"You get used to the small ones after a while." He mindlessly watched the increasingly steady flow of men and women into the bar, both dressed to catch the attention of the opposite sex. Although he continued to scan the room for another face that might capture his attention, in his gut he knew there would be none like Madeline Beaudet.

"When do you think you'll make it into the office? I want to introduce you to the staff."

"I need a few days to get my things unpacked. I couldn't find a pair of matching socks for anything."

"Sure. That's fine. Maybe next Monday, then?"

"Yeah. Maybe." He stood and stretched his suddenly achy, tired muscles. "I think I'll call it a night. Sorry, I'm not much company. Moving wears me out."

"Sure! I understand. I'll see you next week. Give me a call if you need anything."

"Will do." He waited a moment for Stan. "Are you coming?"

"No. I think I'll stay here a while."

"Okay." He turned and left, passing dozens of women on his way out. Leggy blondes in skirts that barely covered their asses, sultry brunettes in body-skimming dresses. None of them held his attention for more than a heartbeat.

Looked like his only company tonight would be a cold shower and cable TV.

*****

Maddy spent every morning the following week wondering when Jace would appear in the office. And every morning she was disappointed. And relieved. No Jace.

She lived her life as normally as possible, focusing on work while employing deep-breathing techniques through the worst of Mr. Richards' tirades. And every night as she vented her frustration about her boss's unprofessional behavior to her friends, they'd lecture her about going out and looking for another job.

Truth was she knew she could do better, at least in the money department. But making a job change was scary. There were far too many uncertainties involved. What if the new job didn't work out? What if she wasn't good enough? What if she didn't catch on? All those what-ifs kept her right where she was, even after the worst of days. At least for now.

Maybe someday the benefits would outweigh the what-ifs. In the meantime, she contented herself with quiet nights at home, Friday nights with her two closest friends, and thanks to The Game, dreams of a trip to the Caribbean.

Finally, after a long workweek, Friday night rolled around, and like every week, the three friends gathered in Maddy's living room. Candace set up the game board on the coffee table and wineglass in one hand, pair of dice in the other, she flopped onto the couch and prepared to make her move. She shook the dice in her fist and tossed them onto the table then moved her game piece. It came to rest on a challenge space, and she glanced at Nic before drawing a card and silently reading it.

Her face went snow white, and Maddy felt herself smiling for the first time in days. "What's wrong?"

"This game is stupid."

"It's too late. You can't back out now. What's it say?" Maddy reached for the card but Candace jerked it away.

"It says you stacked the deck."

"How could I do that? You had the game at your house, and I haven't touched a thing since you got here. Unless you left the card you'd hoped I'd draw last week... You two wouldn't stack the deck against me, would you? My two very best friends!"

Candace chewed on her lower lip. "No, of course not. We love you...would only do what we felt was in your best interest—"

"You did! I knew it! Cheaters. You got what you deserve."

"Damn it, this isn't fair! I want a do-over." Candace drained her glass and reached for the deck of cards.

But, thanks to Maddy's glass of soda, and subsequent superior coordination, she was able to snatch up the cards before Candace reached them.

"No," Nic piped in. "It's only fair, Candace. You have to play what you drew. What's it say?"

Sulking, Candace tossed the card at Nic, who scrambled to catch it. "Go to the nearest lingerie store and model three outfits for the store's customers."

Candace's face turned as red as Maddy's couch. And Maddy couldn't help laughing. The joke was on Candace now.

"Oh, this is good!" Maddy said, gloating in her new sense of victory. "But I wonder why you'd think this would be in my best interest. Lingerie?"

"We felt you needed to come out of your shell a bit. We were going to take it easy on you and pick somewhere that doesn't have a lot of traffic," Nic explained.

"Well, I don't feel like being so 'easy'. I say we hit Victoria's Secret in the mall."

"You're a bitch." Candace stood and headed toward the door. "Better get this over with. The mall closes at nine, and I refuse to give up already."

Maddy, Nic and Candace filed out to Maddy's car, and after insisting she was the only one sober enough to drive safely, Maddy drove to the mall. They walked through the main concourse to the lingerie shop and each made a selection for Candace to model.

Nic was the cruelest. She chose a black corset, panties and stockings. Maddy went for a lovely long silk gown with spaghetti straps, and Candace hid her choice as she strode purposely toward the fitting rooms in the back.

"I can't wait to see what you two draw next, because I'm telling you, paybacks are hell. I'll get both of you. And I won't have to cheat to do it, either."

Maddy knew Candace could, and would, do that. Still, she couldn't help enjoying the moment. Watching her friend, who always seemed so in command of every situation, the friend whose lemons always turned to lemonade. Candace, who was never self-conscious, had to face fear that Maddy could relate to. It was weird, but for whatever reason, it made her feel closer to Candace.

She was human.

Human with cellulite, she noted as Candace strolled out of the fitting room and, with a store-full of eyes glued to her corseted form, waltzed around the room. She stopped in the store's dead center, spun around a couple of times, struck a runway-model-like pose and then headed back to the fitting room.

Maddy and Nic looked at each other, shrugged their shoulders and applauded. And within a heartbeat, the entire store's interior was filled with the sound of applause. And when Candace burst from the fitting room with outfit number two, tastefully chosen by Maddy, the applause swelled. A few male voices injected some hoots into the mix.

Candace lifted her chin, beamed a smile, and looking quite sexy in her shimmery silver gown, walked to the center of the room again. This time, there was a distinct sway in her hips suggesting she was really into it. After striking several poses, she returned to her room and changed. Finally she emerged in a long T-shirt over pajama bottoms, strutted her stuff, took a bow, and waved before returning to the fitting room to re-dress.

She'd done it, and Maddy couldn't help feeling a huge sense of respect for her normally troublesome friend. That had taken guts. Guts Maddy wasn't sure she possessed. In fact, she knew she didn't. How would she ever win this game?

The three friends laughed and chattered as they returned to Maddy's house.

Candace, back to her old, feisty self, pushed the dice toward Nic. "Your turn."

Nic rolled a two. Hopped her game piece two spaces and sat back, smiling. "No Challenge card for me tonight."

Candace frowned. "That's twice. Are you using loaded dice?"

"Nothing's loaded here but you," Nic teased back.

"I'm not loaded, just a little buzzed." Candace turned to Maddy. "Your turn." She smiled.

Maddy counted out the spaces to the next challenge space. "Five. That's either a four and a one or a two and a three," she whispered to Jack, who'd taken residence in her lap again. Any other combination was good. Surely she'd get another combination! She closed her eyes, shook the dice and dropped them.

Thunk. Thunk.

"Whoo-hoo!" Candace shouted. "Challenge."

Startled, Jack jumped from her lap and as Maddy opened her eyes, she watched him shoot across the room to find refuge. Her heart down around her toes, and wishing she could join him under her bed, she glanced at the seemingly benign deck sitting on the coffee table. She'd been lucky with her first draw. Most of the other cards were a lot tougher than the last challenge she'd faced. Hoping her next one wouldn't involve traipsing half-naked around a public place, she reached for the deck, her heartbeat thudding in her ears, and lifted the card to read it.

Her eyes skimmed the print, but the meaning of the words didn't hit her brain until she'd read it through twice.

And then she felt herself heating from the inside out. "No way. I'm not doing this."

"What?" Nic plucked the card from Maddy's weak grip and read it. She grinned. "Oh, this is going to be good!"

"Good?" Maddy repeated. "No, not good. Not at all. Because I'm not going to a bar and asking strangers for their underwear! How gross is that? And how immature? I feel like I'm hazing for a sorority. What if someone I know sees me there? What will they think?"

"Who? Who's going to see you?" Nic asked.

"You never know. Someone from my mother's church, maybe. Mom'd be devastated if she saw me acting like—"

"In a bar?" Candace laughed then drained her glass of wine. Standing, she headed toward the kitchen, saying over her shoulder, "I could just picture your mother's holy roller friends in a bar."

"They might go there to witness. They've witnessed on the beach before."

"Oh, come on! Don't tell me you're giving up already! That's just an excuse." Returning with a bag of chips, Candace shoved a handful into her mouth and chewed. "I waltzed through the mall wearing a leather corset, for God's sake. You can ask a couple cute guys for their underwear."

"What if they aren't wearing any?"

"Then you ask the next guy," Nic answered, helping herself to some chips as well. "What's the big deal? It's for a vacation. We can't make it too easy."

"Easy?" Anger bit her insides. "You haven't had to do a single challenge, yet, Nic. Don't tell me what's easy."

"Here." Candace shoved her newly refilled glass of wine at Maddy. "Drink this and you won't think it's a big deal. Hell, if you drink enough, those church people will be the last thing on your mind."

She pushed the glass away. "No, thanks. You know I don't drink."

"That's part of your problem." Clearly not ready to give up, Candace took a few gulps of the wine and then pushed the glass toward her again.

Knowing Candace would insist, she took it and set it on the side table. "I won't ask what the other part is if getting drunk is a solution in your book."

Candace slipped from her seat on the sofa and crouched in front of Maddy. "Remember, this game is all about taking chances, pushing yourself? That's what you wanted to do. Cast aside your old ways, try something new. After last week, I thought you were ready. You said you wanted to win. What's changed?"

"Nothing. But after what you did, I don't stand a chance. I mean, you deserve to win! That was really something you did in that store. My God, I couldn't have done that."

"Sure you could! You're stronger than you think you are."

"I know I'm strong. That's not the issue." She rummaged through her brain, knowing what question was coming next, and not altogether clear what the answer was.

"Then what is the issue?" Nic scooted forward in her chair.

"It's... Well, I..." *Oh, hell!* "I guess I'm just not in the mood for this tonight." That much was true, even if she couldn't exactly say why she was suddenly in such a blue funk.

Candace shoved the wineglass at her again. "Drink this and you'll be in the mood. In fact, you might even have some fun."

She stared at the glass, and at the clear liquid it contained, knowing it wasn't poison. In the back of her mind, her mother's condemning speech about the damnation of her soul pounded, yet she reached. God didn't damn people for drinking. She'd known that for years. So why was it so hard to shake someone else's beliefs? She gripped the glass in her hand and held it under her nose.

The smell, fruity, sort of spicy, burned a bit. She took a tiny taste, unprepared for the bite after the initial tangy taste. *Ewww...yuck!*

"See? It isn't so bad." Candace filled the glass to the top.

Not bad?

"Of course, you're going to have to drink a lot more than that if you want to get buzzed." She pushed the glass toward Maddy's mouth. "It's not going to kill you. In fact, a little buzz is a lot of fun." She wrapped her fingers around Maddy's and helped her lift the glass to her mouth. "Come on. Take a nice, healthy drink."

"My mother would call you a bad influence."

"You've always known I was a bad influence. That's why you're still my friend. You like a little bad in your life." She tipped the glass until the liquid touched Maddy's lips. "Now, down you go."

Maddy took several big gulps, shuddering at the funny, bitter taste that lingered after the liquid burned down her throat. Kind of like drinking a glass of cough syrup. Then she gasped and pulled the glass away from her mouth. "How can you drink this stuff? It's terrible."

"Finish it off and you won't taste anything anymore."

"Maybe you should ease up, Candace," Nic said, looking a little worried. "We don't want her passing out."

"She's had half a glass. She won't pass out from that." Candace nodded toward the half-full glass. "Finish up, then we'll get dressed and go collect your underwear."

A whisper of curiosity about how it felt being buzzed, as Candace called it, sounded in her head, and deciding she'd give into it, Maddy took a deep breath and dumped the remaining wine down her throat. Would it really be fun?

She set the glass on the table. "When does it start?"

"In a few minutes. Your body has to absorb the alcohol." Candace stood and pulled Maddy to her feet. "Let's get you dressed and get going. It's late, and you have a date with several men's underwear."

Chapter Three

Feeling a little wobbly, her head a little soupy, like the time she took too much cold medicine, Maddy followed Candace and Nic to the bedroom, dressed in the one slutty outfit she owned, the same little black dress and heels she'd worn last time, and headed out the door. By the time she hit the car's backseat, the buzz seemed to have set in, full force.

And she felt downright giddy.

Nic, clearly the only one sober enough to get behind the steering wheel, drove them back to the bar they'd visited last week. And ready to face her challenge head-on, Maddy climbed out of the backseat. Candace was right, it just might be fun.

Yep, a little wine sure did change a person's perspective on some things.

Her friends at each elbow and feeling quite sexy, Maddy strolled into the bar, gave the bouncer a wink as she paid the cover charge, and then walked into the dark interior.

This time, things looked very different. From the moment they walked into the claustrophobic, stifling interior, they were pressed in from all sides by bodies. Males, females. Chattering, laughing, flirting people on the hunt for that elusive significant other, even if only for a night.

As they walked through the first room, a smaller, more intimate bar area, she wondered if Jace was there somewhere. Or in the larger room beyond? In that dark corner, maybe. Waiting for her?

Or with someone else.

Oh…she didn't want to think about that.

How would he react when he saw her? Would he smile and flirt? Or would he be stiff and reserved? They'd parted on such awkward terms last time. She couldn't be sure exactly what to expect.

She had to see if he was there. But before she got more than a step or two toward the main dance room, someone caught her arm and pulled. Hard.

"Where are you going?" Candace asked.

"In there." She pointed toward the double-wide doorway.

"No, you're not. You're going to talk to your first victim." Candace motioned toward one end of the bar. "Over there. He's looking at you."

"Who he? What he?"

"Over there. The cute blond." Candace smiled and licked her lips. "I bet he doesn't wear tighty-whities."

Maddy took a quick glance over her shoulder. No one was looking at her, including the cute blond on the end. In fact, he was clearly looking at someone else. Candace.

"Why don't *you* ask him?"

"Because this is your challenge."

"Nic, tell Candace here I get to pick my own victims—er, guys."

"Fair's fair, Candace," Nic interjected. "She picks her own."

"Finally, a voice of reason." Maddy gave Nic a smile of appreciation. "Thanks. Now." She pulled her arm free from Candace's grip. "I'm going this way." She turned on the sexy sway, well, as best she could considering her sloshy brain and the tippy floor, and headed through the doorway and into the cavernous room that held the dance floor.

Immediately, she was rendered a blind invalid. The fast-flashing strobe lights made the world inside the room a confusing morass of images, faces, lights, and walls. Where was she? Would they turn off that damn light?

She bumped into someone and staggered backward, hitting someone behind her, too. Muttering apologies into the air, she closed her eyes to try to get her balance back and prayed for the lights to quit.

Thankfully, they did, and when she opened her eyes, she was staring straight into a pair of very friendly, very male eyes.

"Don't you just hate those lights?" the ordinary but relatively safe-looking man asked.

"Especially after chugging a glass of wine, yes."

He chuckled, a sound she found fairly pleasant, not nearly as intoxicating as Jace's, but not far behind. "Yeah, I suppose that would make it tougher."

She smiled. Things were going well enough. He seemed nice. Safe. She supposed she could just be upfront and ask for his shorts. Either he'd laugh in her face, call for security, or give them to her. "Can I ask you a strange question?"

His gaze wandered up and down her body, and she had to force herself not to cross her arms over her chest. *Damn dress. My boobs are practically hanging out.*

"Sure." He smiled. "Strange is good."

"Can I have your shorts?"

He looked stunned for a moment, a little dazed. And then he grinned. "Is this a joke?" He glanced over her shoulder then side to side. "Did my asshole buddies put you up to this?"

"Oh, no. *Your* asshole friends didn't. Mine did. So what do you say?"

His smile faded a bit as he studied her face. Then, evidently convinced a camera crew wasn't going to jump out from behind something and broadcast his embarrassment all over the country, or his friends wouldn't howl at his susceptibility to a female, he shrugged. "Okay. Sure."

"It's for a stupid contest." She figured she owed him at least some semblance of an explanation. After all, the man was giving up his skivvies.

"A contest?"

"Yeah. It's a stupid game my friend bought online."

"I thought maybe you were hazing for a sorority." He started walking toward the black-painted far wall where the bathrooms were located, and she followed, winding between dancing, talking bodies.

"I know. It sounds like something college kids would do, doesn't it?" she shouted over the booming music.

"What's the prize?"

"A trip."

"That part sounds nice." He stopped outside the men's room. "Be right back."

"Thanks! Oh, and if you could, can you get a couple other guys in there to hand over theirs as well? I need three."

"Sorry. I'll give you mine. But there's no way I'm asking guys to take off their underwear for me."

"Oh." *Duh!* She felt her face heating. "I hadn't thought of it that way." She giggled. "That was really stupid."

"I'll be right back." He disappeared into the bathroom, and she turned around and rested her back against the wall, hoping maybe she'd catch a couple more men as they walked into the john. What better place was there? In fact, it was genius parking herself right here. She'd have her three pairs in no time.

Donning a casual-but-sexy pose, shoulders relaxed, elbow resting on the narrow, chest-high shelf, on the wall, one hip pushed out a little, she met the gaze of the next guy who walked toward the bathroom. But when he averted his gaze, she figured he was not the ideal target. The next one, however, gave her a lopsided smile after a lengthy once-over.

"Hi," she said, trying to keep herself from laughing at how silly she felt. "Can I ask you for a favor?"

"Sure, doll." He gave her a second up-and-down, making her feel a bit like prime beef in the butcher's window. "Whatcha need?"

"Uh... Your underwear."

He gave her that same stunned expression the other man had given, but then his expression turned downright wicked. "Really?" He stepped closer, and she found herself trying to melt into the wall.

"It's for a game. Uh, what do you say?"

"I'm all for it." He paused, gave her a Cheshire cat smile, and trapped her between two outstretched arms. His palms rested on either side of her shoulders, his body pinning her against the wall. "If you'll take them off me."

Her heart stopped beating.

"Oh, no. Er, I mean..." She ducked under one arm and staggered around him. "That's against the rules."

"Here you go, Cutie," another voice said from behind her.

Grateful for the interruption, she spun around and smiled, taking the first guy's donation with a lot more gratitude than it probably warranted. But considering where she'd been just moments ago, he was her savior.

"I bragged about a gorgeous woman collecting underwear while I was in there. You've got more than a few volunteers coming."

"Really?"

As if on cue, a stream of men exited the bathroom, each handing her a bunched up pair of underwear. Their apparel ran the gamut, from athletic boxers, her personal favorite, to white briefs, to multicolored boxers. Within minutes she had eight, maybe ten pairs, and at least that many phone numbers as well. And she was ready to leave.

That was, until she heard a voice. A deep voice that rumbled inside her belly.

"It's you?"

Balling the underwear up as small as she could, and holding them to her chest, she searched the crowd surrounding her, knowing whose face she would see. "Jace?"

He stepped around a couple guys who had become just a little too friendly for her comfort, and she nearly wept with relief. His gaze dropped to the men's undergarments piled high in her arms then wandered up to her face. He smiled, but his eyebrows hung a little low. "What are you doing?"

"I can explain, although I don't expect you to believe me."

"I'd love to hear this. It looks like it's going to be a doozy of a story, and I could use a laugh tonight."

"Well, be prepared, although I've got plenty of underwear here if you happen to pee your pants."

He chuckled and rested his hand on the small of her back. "Let's get our table."

Oh, she loved the way that simple touch felt. It was intimate. Private. Very sexy. And it left *her* panties needing to be changed.

Ever aware of his presence behind her, she wandered through the crowd toward their table. Their table! He'd said *our table*. She didn't know they had an *our* anything. Table or otherwise.

She felt a little giddy as she took her seat and let him push in her chair. "Thanks," she said a little loudly, compensating for the music thrumming through the room.

He leaned down and said into her ear, "My pleasure."

Goose bumps popped up all over her body, spreading from her neck down, and she fought back a shiver and giggled instead.

He sat. "I wanted to talk about what happened last week. Drink?"

"I…uh, sure. I'll take something fruity. You order. I trust you."

"Okay." He flagged the waiter and ordered a scotch on the rocks and something called Sex on a Beach.

That sounded promising! Looking at this guy, sex anywhere would be downright tasty.

"Last week, I had a wonderful time talking with you," he said once the waiter left to fill their order.

"Yes. Me, too," she jumped in, sounding a little too eager to her own ears. "I mean, I enjoyed meeting you, and finally putting a face to the chicken scratch on my paychecks." *You said that last time. Can't you come up with something better than that?*

Within a heartbeat, the waiter delivered their drinks, and she eyed hers, a small glass, with some reserve. She sniffed, smelling some kind of alcohol, but also fruit. Pineapple? Orange? She took a sip.

Not bad! She took another taste. No, not bad at all. Cool, fruity. Tangy. As she drank the rest, she felt herself warming from the inside out. No wonder they called it Sex on a Beach. Within moments, she felt like she was cooking in the tropical sun.

"That's what I want to talk about."

What? The tropical sun? "Oh?"

"Yes. You see..." He paused, took a big swig of his drink and set his glass on the table. Then he looked at her with the most imploring eyes she'd ever seen on a man. They were charming, and more intoxicating than the drink she'd just downed. *You keep looking at me like that and I'll agree to anything you ask, handsome.*

"I have no idea how to say this."

"Hell. I'm sitting here with a pile of men's underwear. What you have to say couldn't be much harder to understand than what I do."

He smiled, and she felt her insides melting. Damn, he had a gorgeous face! Those sparkly eyes and perfect lips. "True. And you're still not off the hook. I'm dying to hear all about why you're stationed outside the men's room relieving every willing guy of their shorts."

"Now? I'd rather hear what you have to say first."

"Fair enough." He sighed. "We don't know that much about each other, I realize, even though you work for my company. And I know an office affair can get ugly if things aren't clear right from the start."

"Office affair? Is that what we're having?"

"That's up to you, I guess."

Oh, yeah! I'm game, as long as it involves wild monkey sex! Weekends in bed. Walks on the beach. Quiet candlelit dinners. "Oh? Is there more?"

"Well, you see, I was divorced about a year ago. It was an ugly divorce, and I want you to understand that I'm not ready for anything serious."

Not ready for anything serious? Am I implying I am? "What are you trying to say? I'm afraid that Sex on a Beach left me a little loopy. Can you be more specific?"

"Well," He reached across the table and took her hand in his, and a three-alarm fire erupted in her pussy when he squeezed. "I'm saying I'd like to get to know you better."

But… There has to be a but coming. Where is it?

"But I don't want to rush into anything."

Bingo! "Rush? Am I rushing?"

"Don't get me wrong. You're a beautiful woman. Your body. Your face…and your ass." He gave her that fuck-me look again. The one that had made her melt last week. The one she'd dreamed of seeing again…all week long.

Only this time his mind-numbing, pussy-scorching look didn't quite work. Instead, disappointment doused the fire down below as his true intention somehow wound its way up to her brain. She pulled her hand free. "Oh. I get it, I think. So, you're looking for real sex on a beach—or at least in a bed—but nothing more? Ever?"

He nodded. "Don't get me wrong, I'm not against marriage or commitment. The timing's wrong. I just moved. I'm starting my life over again. I'll be traveling a lot."

Timing? That disappointment morphed into something uglier, anger. Her heart started galloping in her chest. She wasn't even sure why. It wasn't like she'd expected a marriage proposal after a pleasant chitchat, or even after they slept together the first time. Still, for some reason she had the feeling the timing would never be right. How often had she heard that excuse before?

She wanted to hear exactly what he meant in plain terms. Her mind couldn't handle any other, not doused in alcohol. "Let me make sure I've got this right. You're looking for an occasional lay, no attachments. No emotions. Just sex. Until you get tired of me and move on to someone else."

"You make it sound so...selfish, so empty."

Because if that's all you'll ever want, it is selfish and empty. So why was she still sitting there? Why was she even considering taking him up on his offer? She'd never been the kind to purposefully look for casual sexual relationships. Never! Thanks to the upbringing she'd normally like to forget. "I've always thought emotionless sex is empty. Isn't it?"

"No. Not always. Look, I'm just asking if we can take our time. Start out slow—"

"In the commitment department. Not in the sex department," she heard herself saying. Boy! What a little alcohol did to her tongue! She never spoke her mind like this. Maybe if she bit that wagging, overactive appendage it would stop long enough for her to figure out exactly what was happening here.

"Okay. I guess you're not interested. I don't blame you. In fact I appreciate your honesty. You're clearly not the type—"

"You don't know what type I am, really. I mean..." She paused, feeling herself getting defensive and upset when it simply wasn't called for. He was being honest, telling her what he could and couldn't do. They were two mature adults. At present, they hadn't done anything. She could easily walk away. Why did she have to get so emotional?

Maybe because she liked him. More than she wanted to. Already. And hearing him use the same tired excuse so many other guys had used in the past didn't sit right. She'd thought he was more together, more sincere, than that. Then again, maybe she'd led him to believe something she hadn't intended.

Everyone knew men grouped all women into two categories—women they fucked and women they married. "I mean, thanks to this stupid game, I think you've got the wrong impression of me."

"What game is that?" He lifted one eyebrow but left the other where it was.

"It's this stupid game my friends insisted I play. Candace bought it, and it involves stupid challenges, like collecting men's underwear in a public place and modeling lingerie in a store."

"Did you do that, model lingerie? And I missed it? Damn!" He slapped his hand, palm down, on the table and gave her a crooked smile.

"No!" Feeling herself smiling right back, she fought the temptation to reach out and touch his hand again. It was so close, and the brief connection they'd shared earlier had been so electric. She raised her gaze to his face. Damn it, he really was cute. Not only did he have a serious, in-charge kind of look that turned her into a puddle of goo, but a playful little boy kind of look, too.

Did she want more than sex? Did she need more? Even the idea of seeing him naked was making her blood simmer. No man had stirred that kind of heat in her, ever. Feeling her panties getting wetter, she shifted in her chair. "I'm playing along because I want the prize, but I'm not enjoying the challenges." *Except for one, meeting you – at least up until now.*

"So, was I one of your challenges?"

She nodded, feeling a little guilty for admitting it. "Kinda. Last week, I had to find the best-looking guy in the bar and get his name and phone number."

"Best-looking? Me?" He looked genuinely stunned, which made him that much more appealing, if that was possible.

Truly, he had to realize what a hunk he was! She'd never seen a guy with such a gorgeous face, at least not in person. The way his dark whiskers made deep hollows under his cheekbones, and the sexy sideburns that cut down the sides of his face. "Quit trying to look so surprised. Yes, you. Are you fishing for compliments?"

The smile that followed was a panty-scorcher. Hot, hot, hot. She needed a cold shower. Now!

"Me? Never." He leaned forward, his gaze riveted to hers. "But I am flattered."

The way he was looking at her, she was in danger of losing her head completely. In the interest of remaining somewhat lucid, she gazed down at her empty glass.

"Would you like another drink?" His deep, low voice hummed in her head then dropped down between her legs where it did things nothing had done in ages.

"I probably shouldn't. I think I've had my limit, unless a buzz gets better than warm tinglies all over and a head that doesn't quite work right."

"Nope. That sounds like the optimum effect."

She heard the chuckle in his voice and looked up, not surprised to see that knee-buckling smile again. *Talk about warm tinglies.*

"So, what do you think?" he asked.

I like warm tinglies, among other things. "Think? About what? That drink's left me pretty much brain-dead." *And hornier than hell!* "I don't normally drink, you know."

"I gathered that." He stood and walked around the table then reached for her. "What do you say we leave?"

"Already? I was just getting…er, comfortable." She squirmed when another wave of heat pulsed between her legs. *Liar. You're about as uncomfortable as a toad on a porcupine.* "Besides, I think my friends have deserted me." She turned to scan the packed room. There was no way she'd ever find them. Not a chance. *Oh, well!*

"That's okay." He scooped up her hand. "I was hoping we'd leave *together*. Maybe play a different kind of game."

Mmmm...sounds wicked. She shoved the whispers of her mother's condemnation out of her mind, stood, bundled up the underwear for her friends' benefit, and took his hand. For one night, she wanted to be wicked.

Chapter Four

You've never taken the safe road, so why start now? Jace hesitated for only a heartbeat before escorting Madeline—still carting around the shorts she'd collected at the bar as though they were a valuable treasure—into his apartment. Yes, he was doing exactly what he'd promised himself he wouldn't do earlier tonight when he'd wandered into the dance club, hoping to bump into her. But even then he'd known, if given the chance, he wouldn't have the strength of will to turn her down.

Who would? The woman was absolutely stunning. And intelligent. And funny.

And adventurous.

He couldn't wait to see exactly how adventurous she was. His closet was full of toys he'd bought but hadn't put to use yet.

His cock swelled, straining against his pants as he opened the front door and she brushed past him to enter.

Damn, she smelled good.

He stepped in behind her and closed the door. He didn't want to put a damper on the mood, but he had to speak before he couldn't anymore. And that point was approaching at lightning speed. "Before anything happens, I want to make sure we have an understanding. Okay?" He tugged on the front of his pants.

"Yes." She spun around and faced him, smiling. "Sex. No strings."

His eyes gathered in every detail, her glittery, dark eyes, the way her lips turned up at the corners into a wicked little grin. Oh, that was a look! He swallowed. Hard. "And you're okay with that."

She shrugged and toyed with the strap on her dress. "For now. Oh, how 'bout scarves?"

His gaze did a nosedive, right to her tits as they were lifted slightly when she pulled. Delightful cleavage rounded at the top of her chest. His mouth watered. "Scarves?"

"Not that I'd know about that kind of thing, but I figured they'd cut less than strings."

What? Cut? Oh… Finally understanding what she meant, he burst out laughing and gathered her into his arms, loving the way her softness molded to him. He dropped a kiss on her head, inhaling the fruity scent in her hair, and relishing the silky feel of it against his lips. "Sure. Scarves." He lifted a hand to coax her head to tip away from him and ran his tongue from the back of her ear down the slender column of her neck. "Would you like to play a game with me?"

She turned her head to look at him and sighing wound her arms around his neck. "Just tell me I don't have to model lingerie in Victoria's Secret." She pressed against his groin suggestively.

He bit back a moan. "Nope." He swallowed as his cock swelled and his balls tightened more. Damn it! He needed to slow things down, or he'd come before he got her into bed.

He hadn't suffered a trick trigger since he was fifteen!

"Only for me, babe. What do you have on under that dress?"

"Why don't you take a look for yourself? I'll tell you this much. I'm not wearing Jockeys."

Knowing he was playing with fire, but unable to stop himself, he slid his arms down, letting his hands follow the curves of her breasts, the narrowing of her waist, and the swell of her hips. He inhaled again and licked his lips, anxious to taste her again as his hands slipped around to cup her ass.

He squeezed.

Oh, shit!

Dizzy with need, he dropped his head and kissed her, completely unable to stop his urgency from revealing itself. His tongue plunged into her mouth as his lips worked over hers. It dipped and stroked, tasting every miniscule bit of her while his hands kneaded her soft backside and his hips ground his cock into her soft belly. She returned his kiss, her lips pliant but her tongue demanding. It stroked his, performing a frenzied dance in his mouth that took his breath away and made him so hard he wanted to howl.

Damn, she was perfect! He had to see her. All of her.

Breathless, he broke the kiss and took her hand, adoring the rumpled, heavy-lidded, swollen-lipped expression she was wearing. "This way." He led her to his bedroom and motioned for her to precede him into the room. The sway of her hips and the way her dress clung to her round ass nearly knocked him from his feet. "Let's play."

*****

Maddy had no idea what he meant by play…well, no specific idea. But in her state of mind, or rather body, it sounded damn promising.

As long as it didn't involve pain she was up for anything.

The ache between her legs was a steady throb now, and her underpants were sopping wet. Never had a kiss knocked her for such a loop! Never had a touch made her so weak-kneed. And never had a look sent her careening toward orgasm! Well, at least not since she was a virgin.

She stepped into his bedroom, not surprised to see a king-sized bed sitting smack-dab in the center. *A playground!* Even in her hazy-minded state, she noticed outside of that massive piece of furniture, the room was nearly empty. The men's shorts she had collected ended up in a pile, forgotten, where she had dropped them when she entered the apartment.

Jace pulled her toward the bed then reached for a remote sitting on top of a dresser. Instantly the room filled with mellow jazz. "How's that?"

She watched him reach over to return the remote to its place. The muscles of his arms flexed, creating bulges and lines. "Very nice."

He smiled over his shoulder. "I mean the music."

"That, too."

He pulled off his shirt, and she dropped back, hoping the bed was still behind her. *Good God, what a body! He isn't real. He can't be!*

Still smiling, he prowled toward her, reminding her of a very naughty…something. Dangerous, yes that was it. "Your turn," he said.

She swallowed. "My turn to do what?" *Lick every inch of that beautiful chest, I hope!*

"How about a game of Truth or Dare?"

"Are you serious?" She giggled, her gaze fixed on the lines cutting across his stomach. Oh, those abs were beautiful.

"Truth or dare?" he repeated, the firm tone of his voice drawing her gaze upward.

He was serious.

Okay. She hadn't played this game since she'd graduated from junior high, but what the hell? Truth or dare with a half-naked man that looked like Jace Michaels couldn't be a bad thing. Still, she'd play it safe…for now. "Truth."

"What do you fantasize about when you masturbate?"

That wasn't safe! "What happened to questions like 'What's the worst thing you did last week?' or 'If you could kiss one person, who'd it be?'" Those questions were safe. Her eyebrows zoomed to her hairline and she gasped. "I can't answer that other question."

He stepped closer until he loomed over her, his waist at her nose level. She stared for a moment at the swelling in the front of his pants and then forced herself to tip her head back to look at his face.

He licked his lips, and she licked hers.

He reached down and slipped one dress strap over her shoulder then the other, and she felt herself pushing her breasts forward, eager for the touch she was certain would come. He pushed on her dress smack-dab between her boobs and it fell to her waist.

Her pussy throbbed. Her eyelids dropped closed. Her nipples tingled, and her mind sang the *Halleluiah Chorus.*

"Surely you can tell me what your fantasy is." His voice was closer.

She shuddered when she felt his breath warming her right nipple. Still he didn't touch her. Dying for a touch, for relief from the tension that was winding her tight as a spring, she arched her back.

"Uh-uh! I'm not touching you—anywhere—'til you fess up. What's your fantasy?"

"Oh..." Desperate to get some oxygen to her asphyxiating brain cells, she inhaled, but his scent, a warm spicy mix of cologne and man, only disabled her brain more. "I can't."

"What are you afraid of?" He blew on her nipple, and she felt herself swaying.

She reached behind her back and tried to steady herself by planting her hands firmly on the mattress. "I'm not afraid of anything."

He blew on the other nipple, and it pulled taut.

Damn it, would he touch her? Only a lick or a nibble. Anything to put her out of her misery. She opened her legs, hoping he'd lean closer and rest his body against her. She felt her skirt, pulled tight when her thighs parted, roll up her legs.

"Now, that's a sight." He groaned, the sound vibrating deep in her belly.

"Touch me. Please." She arched her back more.

"Nope. What's your fantasy? Tell me." His voice came from a lower position, and she lifted her heavy-as-lead eyelids.

Good God! His face was inches from her pussy! He smiled up at her then looked at the black lace panel barely covering the flesh that was now quivering. He blew a stream of warm air, and she parted her thighs wider, willing it to caress away the urgent need pulsing up and out.

Something snapped in her head. That was it! "I fantasize I'm tied up, and my lover is a demanding powerful man. A…a pirate."

"Thank you!" He sounded as relieved as she hoped she'd feel in a moment. "Now, for your prize."

She tensed. Where would he touch her?

Her right breast!

She sighed as his tongue, slick and warm, flickered over her nipple, teasing it to erection. Then he bit, oh so softly, until she groaned and thrust her breast forward. "More! Please, more!"

He chuckled and moved to her left breast, repeating the torture on that one.

He was trying to kill her! He had to be.

"Fuck me."

"Not yet." He stopped the little licks and bites.

"Why'd you stop?"

"Truth or dare?"

"Wait a minute!" She opened her eyes. "It's your turn."

"Okay." He stood and sat next to her on the bed. "Dare."

She smiled. "Why did I know you'd say that?"

He nodded his head, a silent encouragement.

"Hmmm…" *So many possibilities.* "Oh! I know! I dare you to fuck me."

"That'll come. Later." He grinned.

"No fair!" She game him a playful shove and he fell onto his back.

Now that was a tasty sight! She could stare at that wide-as-Canada chest all night long! And whatever was still hiding under those pants…well, that was making her drool already. "Okay. I dare you to do a striptease for me."

"Now that would be my pleasure!" He jumped off the bed, spun around once, and then took his place before her. Then, his hips swaying, but not to the music, he grinned and unbuckled his belt.

The man had no rhythm, at least not when it came to dancing, but his lack of dancing expertise only made him that much more adorable in her eyes. He turned around and wagged his rear end in her face then faced front again and unzipped his pants. Fraction of an inch at a time, he slid his pants down his hips. Lower. Lower. Lower.

He was wearing black athletic boxers that hugged his swollen cock. *Oh! Tell me…or don't tell me…he stuffed those shorts! Holy shit!*

Still giving her a grin that would make any woman swoon, he let his pants slide to the floor, then kicked them off.

She gave him a little hoot of appreciation, and he stepped forward until his belly was inches from her nose. She was itching to lick that picture-perfect stomach, but his gyrating made it impossible. She lunged forward, and he dodged her over and over again until, tired of chasing a moving target, she reached around his hips, grabbed his ass in both her hands, and forcibly stilled him.

"What a woman has to do to seduce you! I want to give you your prize."

"I'm not finished yet." He leaned back, swung his hips a few times, then caught the waistband of his shorts in his thumbs. With the most intense fuck-me look she'd ever seen stamped over his face, he pulled those shorts down one heart-stopping inch at a time.

He hadn't stuffed. That lump was one hundred percent all man.

Oh my!

She knew she was staring, but she'd never, ever seen a cock that huge.

He cleared his throat. "Well? What do you think?"

"I...uh..." *What do I say? Sweet Jesus, it's huge? Did you have surgery or are you natural?*

"Did you like your dance?"

Her gaze still fixated on his swollen cock, she nodded. "Hmmm. I sure did."

"Good. Don't I get a prize?"

"Yes." A moment later she heard him sigh, and she realized he was waiting...for her to give him a prize.

Hell, how could any prize top what was sitting between his legs?

She glanced up at his face and felt the twinge of unease that had fanned out through her body ease. Encouraged by his smile, she reached out, gripped his cock in her hand and squeezed.

He groaned.

Well. That was a step in the right direction.

She leaned forward and flicked her tongue over the tip, and he tangled his fingers in her hair and moaned.

Oh. This was getting good!

She opened her mouth wide and took as much of him in as she could. What a sensation, her mouth so full, the scent of man filling her nose. Overwhelmed, she closed her eyes and twirled her tongue around the perimeter of the head, slurping like she was sucking on a lollipop.

"Oh, Madeline!" Pulling her hair, he tugged her back, away from that wonderful, tasty cock. "That was wonderful."

She glanced up. His face was pink. Tension made his features look different, more severe. His lips were drawn into a tight line. His jaw muscles visibly clenched under the stubbled skin.

"Truth or dare?"

Which to try… Oh, what the hell! "Dare."

"Go into the kitchen and find something in the refrigerator…" He grinned. "To use as a sex toy."

"In the refrigerator?"

"Yes." He caught her hands, and stark naked—a state that man should always be in—he led her through the living room to the kitchen. He opened the side-by-side refrigerator doors. "Pick anything."

One hand holding her dress so it wouldn't fall to the floor, she scanned the refrigerator's few contents. "Not much to go with here." She momentarily considered the peanut butter, but quickly dismissed that idea. "What do you eat? This wouldn't keep a dog alive for a day."

"Most of the time, I eat out."

"Makes sense." Not crazy about the remaining items—a half gallon of milk, loaf of bread and a bottle of water—she went for the only thing she recalled anyone ever using as a sex toy, the ice cube tray. "How about this?" She held it out to him.

"Perfect." Taking the tray from her in one hand, he pulled her back to the bedroom with the other. "Ice can be fun. Ready for your prize?"

"That's it? I don't have to do more?"

He cracked the ice in the tray and nodded. "You'll have to undress, but leave the stockings on. They're sexy."

She slid the dress off, not a difficult task since it was nothing but a bunch of velvet gathered around her waist. Then she slipped off her black lace panties.

"On the bed," he said around an ice cube.

She slid into the middle of the bed and waited, feeling nervous and excited all at the same time. Her pussy was dripping wet, pulsing. And it flamed when he crawled onto the bed with her and pulled her knees apart.

"You're so beautiful. Perfect." He teased her labia with a fingertip, skirting around her outer folds. Her eyelids fell closed in reaction.

And when he slipped that finger inside, her moist walls clamped tight around it.

"So tight and wet."

Something cold and soft touched her clit and she gasped. It circled slowly, and her stomach muscles clenched, tipping her hips up.

"Oh…more!"

He pushed a second finger inside as his cold tongue tortured her clit with a steady rhythm. In and out, in and out went his fingers. Round and round went his tongue. And her body hummed from head to toe. Her mind fell away, and her soul shot from her body, floating high in the sky.

Suddenly he stopped.

Breathless, so close to orgasm she could taste it, she opened her eyes. "What happened?"

He was kneeling between her legs, poised to plunge his condom-sheathed cock inside. On his face was written such urgent needing she had to look away.

"Please," she whispered. "Fuck me now."

His cock pushed at her pussy, and the skin stretched slowly to accommodate his girth. She sucked in a breath, feeling the slight burn as he slid deeper and deeper.

And then he was inside, filling her so completely she didn't want to breathe. She closed her inner muscles around him, and waves of warmth washed over her stomach and chest.

He slowly pulled that magical cock out, and she immediately felt empty. When he plunged it inside again, she gasped.

With each thrust, he drove her wild. Each moment they were joined felt like a lifetime. Every touch inside fed her soul. Every sound, his breathing, his moans of pleasure, fed her spirit.

This was magic.

Her body wound tighter until even her foot muscles were cramped. Her legs spread wider, welcoming his thrusts, until her inner thighs were at their limit. His fingers slid over her clit in rhythm to his thrusts, sending her rocketing toward orgasm.

And then she felt the first wave of heat shoot through her body, and digging her fingernails into his shoulders, she sighed. "Oh…"

"That's it, Baby. Take it. Take me."

She crashed through the torrent of pleasure, her entire body gripped in an orgasm that seemed to last forever. In the back of her mind, she heard his groans as he quickened his pace and found his own release.

And then drawing the first breath she remembered taking for a long, long time. She wrapped her arms around his shoulders and clung to him.

His weight rested over her body as he relaxed. He spread soft kisses over her face and neck, and when she opened her eyes, he smiled.

"That was quite a game, eh?" he asked.

She consciously tightened her pussy around his slackening cock. "Yes, it was."

"I can't wait to play the next one."

"Next one?"

"Yeah. But not tonight. You, my sweet, have worn me out." He slid his cock out, sat up and removed the condom. "Do you need anything before we go to sleep? Something to eat?"

"You have an empty refrigerator, remember?"

"I can order carryout. I want you to keep up your strength. You have no idea what's in store for you tomorrow."

He gave her that heart-shattering grin, and she smiled back.

Oh, yeah. This was going to be the weekend of a lifetime! *Does Monday really have to come?* "Wait! You didn't do your last Truth or Dare."

"Okay." He settled back in bed, pulled the covers over both of them, and gathered her into his arms. He kissed her hair. "Truth."

She hesitated for a moment, not sure how he'd react to her question. But she had to ask. She had to know. "What's your worst fear when it comes to relationships?"

He stiffened slightly against her, and she softly stroked his chest, knowing she had to tread carefully. In her gut, she knew he was hiding something. And that something would hold him back until he dealt with it. Maybe it was too soon to think he'd tell her, but considering what he'd asked earlier of her…

He lifted one arm up and rested his head on his hand. "My father had affairs throughout my entire childhood. My mother tried to cover it up, act like nothing was wrong, but by the time we were in junior high, we knew."

"How terrible."

"Once, I asked him why he did that to Mom. And he told me he couldn't help it. He said he felt guilty as hell every time, but something made him wander."

She had no idea what to say.

"I cheated on my wife. I don't know if I learned it from that bastard or inherited it, but I know if I were to ever get married again it would be a big mistake. I liked being married. I loved my wife. But I couldn't be faithful." His voice shook, and she glanced up into his face.

Such sorrow. Such guilt.

She didn't want to hear more.

"Shelly was devastated. I won't do that to another person." He squeezed her, his arms closing around her in a warm hug.

"I understand." Inside, she wept.

Chapter Five

Two weekends. He'd only spent two action-packed, mind-blowing weekends with Madeline. Why did he feel like he owned her? Hell, he hadn't felt such an overwhelming urge to possess his wife…after a year of marriage!

He tried to ignore the way she smiled at Rob, the new rep they were training this week. She was not flirting!

She giggled and tipped her head as she looked into Rob's eyes.

Shit! She was flirting!

And Rob was eating it up, bastard. Not that Jace could blame him.

Jealousy burned his insides like acid. "Let's go into my office, Robert." He avoided looking at Maddy. Damn he was mad, even though he knew he had no right to be.

"Please, call me Rob."

"Rob. Fine." He opened the door and impatiently motioned him into his office.

I can't give her more. I can't ask for more, he repeated over and over in his head as he followed Rob into the office and closed the door.

His mantra didn't take away the seething anger, and it took every ounce of his self-control to keep from taking it out on the schmuck sitting in front of him. "Let's talk about sales," he grumbled.

"I'd rather talk about Maddy."

Madeline.

"She's cute."

"She's taken."

"She is?" Rob glanced over his shoulder toward the door, as if he half expected her to be standing there waiting for him. "She didn't mention a husband or even a boyfriend."

"Take my word for it."

"I don't know, man. No woman looks at a guy like that if she's happily…uh, taken."

Jace slammed his hands on his desk. "Enough! You're here to train, not to get laid. Got it?"

Rob leaned back and lifted his hands in defeat, his eyes narrowing. "Sure, sure. Train on."

Jace sat back and consciously tried to slow his galloping heart. "Sorry." *I'm an idiot.* "I shouldn't have yelled, but you have to understand this business takes a lot of self-discipline. No one'll be standing over your shoulder making sure you do what you should. Got it?"

"Sure."

"Good."

After a couple of hours going over the spring line, Jace escorted Rob outside to his conversion van-slash-traveling showroom. But before they left for their appointment at a nearby country club, Jace made an excuse and dashed back inside.

He found Madeline at her desk. "I need to talk to you tonight. How about dinner?"

She gave him that smile—the one she'd given Rob a while back. "Sure. That sounds great!"

"Good. See you tonight. I'll pick you up at around seven."

He spent the rest of the day worrying about exactly what he would say. Could he admit how he felt? What did it matter? He couldn't demand a commitment when he knew damn well he wouldn't hold to it. Or could he?

The appointment went as well as it could, considering his mind was elsewhere and Rob didn't know a damn thing about sales, but they left with a decent order. They returned to the office, and Jace loaded samples into Rob's car and sent him back to Indiana. Rob wasn't ready yet to go it alone, but at least he'd have a harder time getting into Madeline's panties if he was hundreds of miles away.

Still uncertain how the night would go, Jace drove to Madeline's house and parked. His palms were sweaty, his face and ears hot.

What this woman did to him!

When he lifted his hand to knock, the front door opened, and a beaming Madeline greeted him.

"Hi." She motioned him inside. "I have a surprise."

He felt a smile pulling at his mouth, even though his insides were tied into knots. "For me?"

"Yes, for you. Who else would it be for, silly?" She took his hands in hers and pulled him inside. Immediately the smell of food filled his nostrils. His empty stomach roared in response.

"What did you do?"

"You seemed a little tense today, so I thought I'd make you something special." She stood on tiptoes and gave him a chaste kiss on his flaming cheek. "You're warm." She scowled and felt his forehead with cool fingers. "Are you feeling okay?"

"I'm fine. It was a long day." Slightly embarrassed by the telltale red face, he shrugged away from her hand. "How did you find time to cook? You just left work."

"It's my secret, and I'm not telling." She smiled over her shoulder as she walked toward the kitchen. "Please tell me you like steak."

"Who doesn't?"

She reached into the oven, and bending over to highlight one of her better assets, thanks to the snug jeans she was wearing.

He couldn't help himself. He ran his fingertips down the center seam of her jeans.

Turning, a plate in each hand, she gave him a playful scowl. "Men. They only think about one thing..." She winked. "...thank goodness!" She set the plates on the table, sat and patted the chair next to her. "You can put those thoughts aside for a few minutes, can't you?"

"You bet. For a few minutes." His gaze tangled with hers for a moment before dropping to the food-laden table. Salad. Steaks that smelled amazing. Baked potatoes with the works. "This looks delicious. Thanks."

"You're welcome." She smiled and took a bite of salad. "You looked upset earlier. I thought this would maybe cheer you up. Did something happen today?"

This was his chance. He could tell her how he was feeling right now. He could say, *Just the idea of you looking at another man drives me crazy. You have to be mine.*

Then the image of his ex-wife's red, tear-stained face cut through his mind.

Or not.

"I was anxious to get Rob on the road. I have some concerns about him."

"Oh." Her shoulders dropped a fraction of an inch...or had that been his imagination? "So, you were upset because you're not sure Rob will work out?"

"Yes. Indiana is a key state. And the owners of Links Outfitters are putting a lot of pressure on us to build up that territory."

"Oh." Dropping her gaze to her plate, she took another forkful of salad. "I thought maybe it was something else."

They ate in silence, and when the delicious meal was over, Jace wasn't sure if he should leave or stay. He tried to feel Madeline out, but she had become a little distant.

She knew he was lying, damn it!

Then another thought shot through his mind. Had she flirted with Rob on purpose? Was she trying to make him jealous?

For a brief moment, anger took rein. Was she trying to manipulate him? Trap him? Then guilt and flattery took the anger's place. She cared enough to *want* him to be jealous.

As she stood at the sink, rinsing dishes, he stepped up behind her and wrapped his arms around her waist. "That was a wonderful meal. Thank you."

"I bought it from Outback," she admitted flatly, obviously upset.

His insides squirmed. Damn it, he hated things being like this between them! He despised the hurt and distance more than he hated watching her flirt with Rob. "I still appreciate it."

She sighed after placing the final dish in the dishwasher and, stepping out of his embrace, turned to face him. "Tonight wasn't what I thought it would be."

"Is it my fault?"

"No. It's mine." Her lip trembled, and he lifted a fingertip to try to still it.

She pulled away. "Please don't."

"Tell me what's wrong."

"Nothing's wrong." She sniffled.

"You're crying. Why?" He reached out and gathered her to him. "Please tell me."

She sagged against his body, sniffling and swiping at her tearing eyes. Still she didn't speak.

Instead she tipped her head up and pulling on his neck silently begged for a kiss.

And being a man who couldn't resist Madeline's pleas, he obliged.

The kiss was soft, tentative. Her lips trembled under his, and her body shook as it pressed against him. Tiny choked sounds rose from her throat and filled his head. Still, wrought with guilt over the hurt he was already causing her, he kept kissing her. His lips worked softly over hers. His tongue slipped into her mouth and slowly tasted her. And just as slowly, the whimpers stopped and the trembling stilled.

And, as the kiss became more urgent, his cock raged to life, pushing on the front of his pants.

Her breathing quickened and her tongue plunged into his mouth, twisting and mating with his. Her fingers tangled in his hair, her fingernails scratching his scalp.

When he dropped his hands to knead her breasts, she gasped and broke away, pulling on his neck until he stooped and pressed his pelvis hard against hers.

Gritting her teeth, she set her gaze on his and ground herself into him. "I need you," she whispered.

"I'm here for you, baby." He reached out to hug her again.

She shook her head. "No. I need all of you." She pulled back, unzipped his pants, pushed down his underwear and gripped his cock in her hand. Instantly dizzy, he caught himself before he fell over.

Backing himself against the wall, he stood on quickly weakening legs as she kneeled before him. His heart swelled at the sight of her on the floor, stroking his cock, her beautiful eyes gazing up at him, pleading with him to love her.

His soul cried out for release from the cage he'd built around it.

His mind fortified the lock.

"Please. Give yourself to me." She ran her hand up and down his cock, and he felt his hips thrusting in the same rhythm. "Forgive yourself. Let yourself love again."

No. I'll hurt you. "I'm afraid."

She opened her mouth and took his cock inside, and his head dropped back, banging against the wall. The resulting thud did nothing to diminish the raw pleasure her mouth gave him. Sounds were magnified. The music of loving, slurping, kissing, flooded his mind, washing away all other thoughts. Her warm, wet mouth slid in a steady motion from base to head and back down again, and every muscle inside him tensed. He felt himself heating from the inside out, weakening, as need and dependence took over his body and spirit.

"I need you, too," he heard himself mutter.

She stopped and he looked down.

The smile that greeted him fed his spirit like nothing ever had.

And he knew in that instant he was falling in love with her. Already.

He was in for heartbreak. And so was she. If only it could be avoided.

He had to protect her.

She stood and took his hand, twining her fingers between his. "Make love to me."

Unable to speak, lost in a whirlwind of thoughts and feelings, he nodded. Doubt and desire tangled with relief and fear. Joy danced with sorrow. Indecision jumbled with certainty. He followed her into the bedroom and stood, mute and lost, in the middle of the room.

She gave him an encouraging smile and pulled her shirt over her head. He fought to keep his gaze on her face, knowing what beauty lay just south of it.

"You are the most incredible man I've ever met."

He tried to speak, tried to deny what she said, but his throat was closed tight. *I'm not special. I'm a bastard.*

"You're strong. Sexy. Caring…"

If I were so strong and caring I'd leave now and spare you a heap of pain. Last weekend we fucked. But this is different. If we make love now… Oh, damn it, I'm weak!

"You're intelligent, driven, decisive."

Decisive?

"Look at me. Do you want me?"

Hell yes!

"Am I beautiful enough for you?" Her lip quivered, and the invisible grip on his muscles released. Finally able to move, he lurched forward and pulled her to him, wrapping her in a tight embrace. He dropped his head, his cheek resting on the top of her hair, the smell of delicate, sweet flowers filling his nostrils.

"Yes. You're the most beautiful woman in the world."

She made a funny sound, maybe a giggle and a sob in one, and he squeezed her harder.

"You're absolutely perfect in every way."

"Make love to me." She pulled out of his arms and back-stepped toward the bed, unzipping her jeans as she walked. "For just this moment, I want all of you. Mind, body, and spirit."

You have that already. You have that for always.

She slid her jeans down her narrow legs, and kicked them off. His gaze dropped to the black lace triangle covering her pussy. He felt his already weak resolve evaporating.

And then she turned around, showing him her beautiful, firm ass. One thin line of black lace wrapped around her waist and another plunged between her ass cheeks.

Oh, shit! His knees buckled.

She leaned over the bed, slowly swaying her hips from side to side. "I bought this for you. Do you like it?"

He crossed the room in a heartbeat, pulled her cheeks apart with his hands and ran his tongue down the line of her thong, inhaling her scent as he neared her pussy.

Damn, she smelled like heaven! His balls tightened, and one thought filled his mind, humming through his body like an electrical current. *I must have you.*

She sighed as he pushed two fingers into her slick pussy, and he dropped to his knees. She tipped her hips and spread her legs wide, and he lost his breath. She moaned his name, and what remained of his self-control snapped.

Standing, he rolled her over, pushed her knees up and out and pulled aside the sodden thong. And in the time it took to take a single breath, he was buried deep inside her pussy.

Overcome, he tipped his head back and groaned long and low. Her inner muscles gripped him, almost pulling him deeper. He dug his fingers into her thighs and pulled out slowly until he couldn't stand it and had to thrust deep again.

Her soft moans were the most intoxicating aphrodisiac. They zapped along nerve endings, setting mini-blazes all over his body. Reeling, he gulped in a deep breath, in the process drinking in her sweet essence until he was giddy and dizzy.

With one hand he reached between her legs and pushed aside her thong to stroke her clit, slow, soft, rhythmic, absorbing every minute response to his loving. She sighed and gasped. Her body released that intoxicating scent that nearly drove him crazy with need. Her muscles tensed under his fingertips.

This was loving. Giving and receiving. Sharing. And he knew he didn't want to share this with anyone but Madeline again.

I want to love you. I have to love you. He looked upon her, her spirit and soul fully revealed to him as if her body was transparent.

"Oh, God!" she cried out, tossing her head and reaching out to grip the sheets in her fists.

And then he felt it, the spasms of her orgasm as she milked him. He stilled for a moment, closed his eyelids, halted his breathing, wishing the moment would last forever. And then his body followed hers over the crest, soaring to the heavens and beyond.

When they'd both landed firmly upon the earth, he slipped onto the bed with her and held her, relishing the way her body fit with his, the scent of sex all around them. The sound of her soft breathing.

She squeezed his shoulder and sighed. "Jace Michael…I know you probably don't want to hear this, but I…I'm falling in love with you."

His heart stuttered and his throat clogged.

He'd known it was so. How could he not? Hell, he felt the same way.

But if he told her that, it would be over for her. He had to help her protect herself.

"Aren't you going to say anything?" She propped herself up and gazed into his eyes. "I'm falling in love with you. We just made love. What are you thinking?"

"I'm thinking we need to take things slow like we talked about, okay?" *Shit! I sound like such a cold prick! Damn it all to hell!*

"That's it? That's all you have to say?"

So drowsy he could hardly keep his eyes opened, he shook his head. "I'm sorry, babe. But I've been honest about this from the start. I told you I couldn't handle anything serious. I can't say what you want me to…that I feel the same way. I just can't."

Chapter Six

She wanted to get out of that bed and leave, walk away from him forever…or as it was, shove him out of her bed. Out of her house. Out of her heart. But her heart wouldn't let her do it. The damn thing was so weak, so freakin' pitiful, it wouldn't let her cut the strings binding her to Jace now before she really suffered. Truth was it was already cracking and crumbling into pieces.

Where was that roll of duct tape when she needed it?

Staring at his back as he slept, Maddy cursed herself for getting into this situation. Her pussy was still twitching with aftershocks. Her lips still tasted of his kisses. And his empty words still rumbled through her head.

I told you I couldn't handle anything serious. I can't say what you want me to…that I feel the same way. I just can't.

She was such an idiot! If only she hadn't agreed to play that stupid game, then she wouldn't have groped Jace in that bar, and he wouldn't have seen her in that slutty little dress, and he probably wouldn't have given her the time of day at work…

And her heart might still be in one piece.

She listened to his soft snoring and wondered how he'd become so guarded. She imagined him as a little boy, listening to his parents fight. As a young man, cheating on his wife.

Had he really done that? How often? Was he as bad as he said?

She slowly pulled away from him, and he rolled over and grumbled in his sleep.

He looked so damn sweet. He acted so damn sweet…when he wasn't trying to hide himself from her. How could this same man break his wife's heart?

She gave herself a mental bitch-slap. Enough! Enough games. Enough pretending just sleeping together was all she needed. It was time to be honest with him and herself.

This wasn't good enough. She wanted more. She needed more.

And she couldn't hold him responsible for her feelings. Like he said, he'd been honest, straightforward. It was her choice to agree to his terms.

Why can't I be content? Why do I have to stir things up, make demands! He's a wonderful, giving lover. Why can't that be enough?

Because it plain isn't, and you knew that from the beginning.

She quietly dressed in pajamas and left the room, taking a spare blanket and pillow with her. It was better for both of them if she cut it off now, even if it burned her like a bath in boiling acid.

Yes, this was for the best.

*****

Maddy woke some time later, wondering if he was still sleeping in her bed. Curious, she tiptoed down the hallway.

The door was open.

The bed was empty.

She curled up under the covers, bedding that housed his scent like her mind stored memories, and fighting tears, she forced herself back into dream world. Today, of all days, that was much better than reality. She'd sleep her misery away, if it took her all day.

But later she heard the phone ringing. And even later, she heard pounding on her front door.

The doorbell jangled like its wires had been crossed, unceasing, infernally insistent, until she answered it.

Nic and Candace. She should have known.

Stepping aside, she let them in. They both eyed her suspiciously and grimaced.

"What's up? Have you been sleeping all day?" Candace asked, tugging on Maddy's robe. "Go jump in the shower and get cleaned up. We have another round of The Game to play tonight."

"I'm not feeling well. You two'll have to play without me."

"Are you sick?" Nic laid the back of her hand on Maddy's forehead.

Seeing a way out, she said, "Yes. Deathly. In fact, you both should leave before you catch it." She coughed for effect.

"You don't feel feverish." Nic pulled her hand away.

"I…took some medicine."

"You're full of shit. Let's go. I'm not going to let you get away with this. You'll thank me later." Candace pulled Maddy into the living room. "Now, you can either go clean up and make yourself presentable, or you can face whatever challenge you draw in your bathrobe and bed head."

"I told you, I'm not playing tonight. It won't kill us to take a weekend off."

"Yes, it will. We agreed to play until the Game is over. And you need to get over him now. Staying in bed all weekend won't help." Candace pulled out the board and pointed at the pieces of tape marking their last positions. "We're not even close to finishing the Game."

"I'm through. I've had enough. You two can continue. In fact, here…" She stomped back to her bedroom, grabbed a notebook and pen, and returned. She scribbled the words "I forfeit" on the top piece of paper, signed it, ripped it off, and handed it to Nic. "I told you, I'm through with this ridiculous game. I never should have agreed to play along in the first place. I'm not interested in changing, in trying new and exciting things. My life is perfect the way it is."

Nic glanced down at the paper then at Candace. "Maybe she really is sick. Maybe she'll change her mind later, when she's feeling better—"

"I doubt it." Candace stood, crammed the game board back in the box and headed toward the door. "I know exactly what this is all about. She's not sick. She's just miserable, wallowing in her misery. It isn't healthy."

Nic spun around, facing Maddy, and stopped walking mid-stride. "Miserable? Have I missed something?"

"Yeah," Candace said, gripping the front doorknob. "Only a couple weekends of wild sex."

Nik gasped, her wide-eyed gaze hopping back and forth between Candace and Maddy. "Wild sex? Who? When?"

"Maddy here's been doing her boss for the past week."

"Shut up, Candace," Maddy growled, not appreciating the judgmental tone in Candace's voice.

"I don't know all the details," Candace continued, "but knowing our Maddy, he's only interested in something casual, and Maddy wants a ring and a proposal."

"You don't know anything."

Candace's eyebrows became lost under her shaggy bangs. "Really? I want to hear why you're still in your pajamas then. This has after-sex regrets written all over it. You did the same thing the last time a guy—"

"For your information, I'm perfectly happy with the arrangement we've made. Yes, he's my boss, but we're both adults. We can separate work and play. And I'm the one holding back. He wants more." *If I was Pinocchio, my nose would be miles long, but that ought to shut her up.*

Candace froze.

Now, that's better.

She glanced at Nic, who stood gape-mouthed in the middle of the living room. A heartbeat later, Nik seemed to break out of her spell and smiled. "Wow, Maddy! That's great. You've finally figured out what you want and went for it. Good for you!"

If you only knew. "Thanks." She motioned toward the door. "And speaking of what I want... I'm tired, and I hope I don't have to explain why..." She tugged at the front of her robe and tightened the belt. "So I'm asking you both to please leave. I want to get some rest."

"Sure thing, Maddy." Nic kicked into gear, opened the door, and pushed Candace out. "Call you later!"

"Have fun finishing up the game. I hope you win, Nic." As soon as the front door was closed, Maddy sagged onto the couch.

Did she really believe what she'd said? Could she really accept things as they were with Jace?

The thought of losing what little she had with him was almost unbearable. Maybe she wouldn't get a ring and a proposal anytime in the near future—not that such a thing was even realistic—but at least for a while longer what they had could be tolerable—more than tolerable, she silently corrected, recalling the lovemaking they'd shared last night.

Having him in her bed was better than an empty bed.

And an empty heart.

Going for the phone, she resolved to call him. He had to hear it. She had to say it. If she couldn't have more, she'd take weekends in his arms.

She was pushing them both too hard. It was time to stop.

Chapter Seven

"You're telling me I can get past this? That...that I can stop?" He felt the weight of a dozen elephants lift from his shoulders. *I can commit? I can love!*

"Obviously, I'm making some assumptions, since we've only been talking for a little under an hour. But based on what you've told me today, I believe you can. If you're willing to work on it," the counselor answered with a slow shake of his head. He leaned back in his chair and propped an ankle on his opposite knee.

The man sure looked confident. Could it be true?

Jace didn't know whether to laugh or cry. This was the last thing he'd expected to hear this morning. Counselors didn't cure people, especially after only one visit. They were just a sympathetic ear...or so he'd always believed.

The gentleman sitting across from him smiled under his bushy beard. "You're surprised?"

"Yes, I am. You know the saying, 'Once a cheater, always a cheater'."

"That's a cliché, not an absolute truth."

"When it came to my old man it was."

"From what I see here, you're not your father."

"No. But I'm half him. I saw what he did to my mother. I had to have learned something from that."

"You're not destined to be a cheater just because your father was...unless you truly believe you are. It's a self-fulfilling prophesy."

"I've heard of that. But what does the cure involve? Shock therapy? Drugs?"

"Nope. Nothing that drastic. No wires. No pain." The counselor removed his metal-framed glasses and polished them with a tissue. "There is no cure. You work through the beliefs lying below the behavior, and your behavior will change."

His entire body crawling with excess energy, Jace jumped from his chair and began pacing. "When do we begin?" *Now! Tell me now!*

"You already have. Coming here today is a big step. And having faith in what I'm telling you, too. We'll talk more next week."

"You're going to make me wait a whole week?"

"This isn't something we can do in a single session. It's going to take some time."

"Sure. Okay." He forced his heart to slow down, or tried to. It didn't listen.

"I understand your impatience, but believe me, it's better to take our time."

"Is it bad? Uh, this problem with cheating? I mean I still feel terrible about it. I'll never forget the expression on Shelly's face the day I told her. I couldn't believe I'd hurt her like that. How can I possibly stop? I don't want to do that again, to any woman." *To Madeline.*

"From what I see today, I am fairly certain it's a behavior you can overcome. You just need to change some of your beliefs about yourself."

Thank God!

He stood and motioned toward the door. "We'll see you next week, then. Same time. Same place."

"Yes. I'll be here. Thanks, Doc." Jace gave the man's hand a solid shake before heading out the door.

"Call me if you need anything."

"Will do."

Jace left the building feeling lighter than he'd felt in years. It was as if gravity had lifted and each step sprung him high in the air.

The air smelled sweet. The birds were singing. Life was good.

He headed to his car, anxious to give Madeline the good news. But, *Guess what? I was wrong? I want more with you, now that I know I'm not destined to be a cheating jackass,* just didn't seem to be good enough.

More. He had to do something more. But what?

What would prove to her how much he cared for her? How could he ever hope to deserve her?

As he drove toward work, his mind buzzing, replaying the many conversations they'd shared, the quiet moments, and the crazy ones too, one moment, one sentence, stuck out.

Her fantasy. He could live out her fantasy, right down to the pirate costume.

He'd declare his feelings and take her hostage, fulfilling her every secret desire, until she agreed to be his.

Yes, that should do it. But he needed to prepare. He called the office and told Stan he wouldn't be in. Then he headed home.

Yes, there were preparations to make. Many, many preparations.

*****

Maddy glanced at the clock for the umpteenth time in the last hour. Just past ten. He was supposed to be in the office at nine. She'd tried his cell phone and his home phone. No answer. Something was wrong, or he was purposefully ignoring her calls.

A blade of ice-cold pain stabbed her in the belly. That had to be it. Both phones had caller ID.

In silent misery, she worked straight through lunch. The fact that the office was empty except for her only made it worse. Mr. Richards wasn't expected back for several hours, not that he was welcome company. Keeping her mind busy was her best option, since crying was the only alternative. And no way in hell would she let Mr. Richards see her cry.

At four-thirty on the dot—like always—Maddy heard the office's outside door swing shut and turned to prepare her daily package for UPS.

"Arrr…I've 'eard there's a lovely maid 'ere whose beauty surpasses all the seven seas," a man said in an exaggerated gravely voice.

That's not the UPS guy. Since when does UPS employ…pirates? Was it Halloween? She checked the calendar, then, not sure what to expect, she glanced over her shoulder.

Who was that? What was that? Why?

As his voice suggested, the man standing on the other side of her desk was dressed in the ragtag garb of a pirate. He looked like a Greek Johnny Depp, right down to the beard, hat and long hair.

Absolutely scrumptious.

And then she realized who he was and her eyes burned with joy-filled tears. But before she could speak, or laugh or cry, he swept her into his arms, grabbed her purse and carried her out the door.

She inhaled, surprised to catch the scent of the sea in his clothes. Salt and wind and man. It was a heavenly combination, and delightfully unexpected since the ocean was thousands of miles away. She inhaled a second deep breath. "Where are we going? Should I invoke the right of parlay?"

"You can invoke anything you like, lass." He waggled his eyebrows. "But you're still my prisoner. Savvy?"

She giggled and nodded. "Savvy."

He toted her out to his car and settled her into the passenger seat, bending low to look her eye to eye. "I can trust you not to do anything foolish now, can't I? Or I'll be forced to tie you to the mast." Then he walked around the front of the car, grinning at her through the windshield.

She glanced around the car's interior. "What mast?"

He slid into the driver's seat and smiled. "Use your imagination."

That wicked grin set her blood on fire.

He shifted the car into gear and drove a short distance to a secluded cabin. From the front, she could see the shimmer of a small lake behind it.

"Oh, this is lovely."

He gave her an exaggerated sigh and pulled a toy sword from the backseat. "You're supposed to be scared. Remember, I'm the big, bad pirate. Now, be a sport and play your part."

This was too funny! Anxious to see how far he'd take it, she tried to play along. "Oh, my, Mr. Pirate, please don't—"

"Captain Jace to you, missy." He got out of the car, shoved the sword in his belt, and went around to open her door.

"Oh, yes. *Captain* Jace. Forgive me," she said in an intentionally mocking tone. She accepted his hand out and gave a surprised yelp when he grabbed her and threw her over his shoulder.

He gave her a playful swat on the rear end as he walked into the cabin, and she yelped again. "You, missy, need to learn some manners."

"And a pirate—a lecher and thief—is the one to teach them to me?"

"That and a few other things." He slammed the cabin's front door and locked it, then carried her back to the only bedroom and dropped her on the bed. The aged springs squeaked as her weight bounced on them. His expression a mask of seduction, he climbed on with her, pushing her slowly onto her back. On knees and outstretched arms, he hovered over her, his gaze slowly dropping from her face to her breasts and continuing lower. "Weeks at sea do treacherous things to a man."

"Really?" She squirmed a little as her body heated under his wandering gaze.

"Aye. It isn't natural for a man to be without his woman for so long."

"His woman?" she repeated.

He lifted a hand and traced her lips with a fingertip, then followed the line of her neck down to the first button of her blouse. With agony and desire blazing in his eyes, he unfastened each button and peeled first one side of her blouse away from her body then the other. He bit his lip as he stared at her breasts, pleasantly enhanced by her white lace push-up bra. "Damn!"

Her heartbeat raced, and she gulped air into her straining lungs. Her pussy burned with the need to be filled, soaking her panties.

He dropped his head and, gently pushing her breast up, teased her nipple as it peeked out from under the bra's demi-cup. "You're the most beautiful, amazing, intelligent, giving woman I've ever met. Today is for you. Every moment."

"I had no idea pirates could be so…gentle." She arched her back and pushed her breasts higher. "Harder."

"My pleasure, milady." He cupped both breasts in his hands and squeezed, kneading them roughly, and she bit back a cry of relief.

Oh yes! More!

As if he could read her mind, he pulled her nipple into his mouth and suckled. His tongue swirled around it, and his teeth nipped softly, sending wave after wave of pleasure-pain through her body. She tensed as fevered need spread throughout, heating her from the inside out. And aching to feel his weight between her legs, she caught his hips in her hands and pulled until he rested between her legs.

Her breasts abandoned in favor of her stomach, Jace licked and kissed a blazing trail down, down, down to her lower stomach. The muscles below the skin he touched clenched and she moaned in agony.

Blind, her eyelids too heavy to keep open, she pushed his hat off his head and wound her fingers in his hair. "Oh, yes!"

"Would you like me to love you?" he murmured.

His words stoked the fire within, and she groaned, "Yes! Please. Now." Her hips rocked in pace with the throbbing between her legs, rubbing her pussy against his hip bone. "Please," she repeated when he didn't move.

He caught her wrists and pinned them to the bed, high over her head. "Open your eyes," he commanded.

She fought to do as he asked, but she was so weak and lost in ecstasy.

"Do it now."

Finally, with success, she forced them open and stared into his flushed face.

His expression was such an odd mix she couldn't quite read it.

"What's wrong?" she asked, her hips still rocking back and forth. Her heart hammered out each beat in her ears, and her blood pounded through her body in tidal waves. This man, this wonderful, giving, playful man, needed something from her. But what?

"Would you let me love you forever? I'm not perfect. I have my problems. But I want to work them out, and I want you by my side through all of it. Is that too much to ask?"

Her heart climbed into her throat, and she struggled to speak, knowing every beat of silence was probably torture for him. "I... Oh..." She felt the sting of tears in her eyes, and pulled her wrists free to wipe them away. "I would be honored to stand at your side."

"I hope you're a patient woman, because I'm impossibly stubborn. I'll push you to the bitter end of your rope."

"I'm no angel either, but we can do the best possible for each other. That's all I want."

He smiled, and his lip trembled barely enough to be noticeable. "I don't know what I did to deserve you."

"Be you. That's all. And the pirate getup doesn't hurt." She smiled and motioned toward her pants. "Now, are you going to ravage me, you sexy pirate? Or am I going to be left with my fantasies only?"

"Aye!" In one swift motion, he yanked off her pants and underwear. And kneeling on the bed, he lifted her legs and pushed two fingers inside while teasing her clit with his tongue.

Breathless and dizzy, her body rocketing toward completion, she reached over her head and fisted the bed's coverlet. What he did to her body! And her mind and her spirit.

She heard the soft shuffling sound of his movement, the rip and crinkle of a condom wrapper, then groaned as his cock pushed at her folds.

"I won't ever hurt you. You're mine now, and I'll love you until the day I die." In a heartbeat, he thrust inside her, filling her so completely she gritted her teeth against the urge to cry out.

And as he pumped in and out, carrying her toward the most powerful climax she'd ever experienced, he repeated his promise over and over. "I'll love you forever. I'll love you forever."

They found their release together, their bodies, spirits and voices joined. And afterward, they held each other, crying, laughing and singing.

"Yo ho ho. A pirate's life for me."

And that night, as Maddy lay next to Jace, listening to the birds and woodland animals scamper about outside, she laughed.

Who would've thought a silly man-chasing game between girlfriends would have led to the most amazing, fantastic, wonderful game of all—the game of love.

She'd won, no matter how anyone looked at it.

Master, May I?

Chapter One

Britt Olson knew what her fiery best friend's first words would be the minute she was welcomed inside but she opened the front door anyway. There was no getting around it. She'd have to deal with Mary's disappointment—at least until the package they were both anxious to open was located.

Damn postal system. Even armed with full online package tracking capabilities, Britt hadn't been able to figure out what had happened to her gift, lovingly chosen, paid for, and shipped by her mother. Of course, the fact that Britt hadn't bothered to do more than turn on her birthday gift to herself—a new desktop with all the latest bells and whistles—and play a couple of games of Spider Solitaire, probably didn't help any.

But that game was addicting! A lot more fun than trying to figure out IP addresses and work through tedious connection wizards.

"So, where is it?" Mary asked, her freckled face and pale blue eyes full of expectation. "I came prepared." She stepped inside and dropped a large duffel bag on the floor. It landed with a respectably loud thud.

"Sheesh! What's in there? And what are you preparing for?" Curious, Britt glanced at the worn, blue bag before returning to the kitchen to get their drinks.

Mary followed her. "Oh, you'll see. I have a little bit of everything in it. I didn't want to get caught unprepared. So where's your package? I'm dying to see."

"How about you give me a hint first?" Britt struggled with the corkscrew, silently reminding herself of a recent vow to purchase a better one. "I think it was rotten of my mother to tell you what she bought—"

"You want some help?" Mary reached for the bottle.

"No. I'm fine. I'll get it." Britt gritted her teeth and continued pulling on the stubborn cork. "The hint, please."

"I think your mom wanted to make sure you didn't have it already."

"It? What it?"

Britt bit her lip as Mary gave her an I'm-not-telling-smile and shrugged. Prying information out of her best friend was no easier than pulling the cork out of the bottle she held between her knees.

"This isn't fair. You're more excited than I've ever seen you. More excited than the night before you moved into your new house, more excited than the day before you started that nifty new job of yours. Come on! Just one teeny, tiny hint."

"Nope. I'm not talking. Now, where is it? You promised not to open it 'til I got here. So quit with the theatrics."

"Fine. I see how you are. Just wait 'til your birthday." The cork finally slid free of the bottle and Britt smiled in triumph. "As far as where the box is... Well, um..." She poured Mary a glass of wine and handed it to her. "I'm not sure."

Mary didn't bother to hide her disappointment as she glanced at her watch. "It's after seven. You should have gotten it by now. Your mother always has your presents delivered on your birthday. She promised me—"

A resounding knock startled both women, and they simultaneously looked at the front door.

"Are you expecting anyone tonight?" Mary asked.

"Nope."

A second loud knock sent them both scurrying toward the door. Britt peered through the peephole.

It couldn't be. Why would he be here? She blinked then looked again. "It's the guy who bought my house. Andre. Should I open the door? What if he's mad about the bathtub faucet? Or the crappy back door that barely closed. Or the—"

"You sold that dump 'As Is'. You gave him a full disclosure. He has no right to come over here angry. Does he look mad?"

Britt studied his features—slightly contorted by the peephole's curved lens, but still stunningly handsome—for a few seconds. She'd never gotten this close to Andre Manuel Cruz-Romero, better known as Andre Romero, before. Funny the things a person learned about a total stranger during the lengthy process of closing on real estate. She knew practically everything about him but his measurements.

And there were a few of those that she wouldn't mind knowing—specifically the length and girth of one part. She hadn't been able to ignore the sizeable lump in his trousers during the closing meeting last week.

The slightly magnified effect of the lens gave her a great opportunity to see the olive-skinned hunk up close—well, at least his face. There were the most amazing gold streaks in his deep brown eyes. A sexy mole sat high on one cheek. Dark stubble lined his jaw and covered his chin. And his curly hair frolicked over the top of his head in a flirty wave flopping over one eye. "No, he doesn't look mad. Just a bit impatient." She turned the deadbolt and opened the door. "Hi, Andre. What a surprise."

Perfect, white teeth flashed brightly against his warm, brown skin. "Hi. You had a package delivered to the house today. I thought it might be important. I hope you don't mind but I signed for it." He thrust a decent-sized cardboard box toward her.

"Oh! Thanks! I don't mind at all. My mother must have forgotten." She glanced at the label then up into his eyes. "That was very sweet." *My God, he's handsome. Look at that mouth! I bet he's an amazing kisser*. She held in a sigh and tried to remember what she'd been saying.

Too late. It was gone.

"It's a birthday gift," Mary said, clearly trying to cover for Britt's major brain fart.

"Really?" he said, those perfect lips pulling into another perfect smile that held just a hint of danger. He leaned closer, and for some reason, Britt felt sure he was going to kiss her. She closed her eyes and held her breath. "Happy birthday, Britt," he whispered.

Nothing touched her lips but a soft puff of air. *Damn! No birthday kiss?*

Feeling really stupid, she opened her eyes. What had made her think he'd kiss her? While they knew a lot about each other, thanks to the load of paperwork they'd signed a week ago, they were still virtual strangers. After all, it had been a property closing, not a date that had brought them together for a couple of hours.

"Would you like a glass of wine?" Mary offered, giving Britt a nudge.

Coming to, Britt motioned him inside and stammered, "Yes, please. You're welcome to come in. It's a little chilly outside." *You're welcome to do more than that, but sharing a glass of wine's a nice start.*

"Okay, but just one." He stepped inside and took a visual tour of her living room. "Nice place." To his credit, he didn't compare it to the shack she'd sold him.

Still, she had an irresistible urge to explain why she'd sold him a house that was in such rough shape. "Thanks. This place is more my speed. I tried to fix the old place up, but it was too much for me. It belonged to my grandparents, and I loved the old farmhouse, but I'm just not capable—"

He lifted a fingertip and pressed it to her lips. "No need to explain. The house is old and it needs a lot of work. I'd never expect anyone—even a woman who seems as capable as you—to be able to tackle it on her own."

Stunned into silence by the innocent, yet provocative, touch to her mouth, she stared into his eyes and forced herself to resist the urge to tease his finger with her tongue then pull it into her mouth and suck.

His very sexy and dangerous expression made her tingle all over. She felt her panties getting wet.

Only when he pulled his finger away was she able to speak. "I...own a Dewalt, cordless...you know."

He reached for her again, this time seeming to aim for her shoulder. His gaze slipped from her face.

She tensed up with expectation.

But his hand never made contact with her. Instead he smiled at someone or something behind her and said, "Thanks." Then, pulling his arm back, and leaving her to watch the way his biceps thickened as he moved, he brought a glass of wine to his mouth and sipped. His tongue darted out as he lowered the glass. "Mmm. Very good wine."

"Yes." She tried to slow her panting breaths, sure she sounded like a dog.

"So, you were saying you have a Dewalt? That's impressive. I don't know many women who—"

"Would you like to have a seat?" Mary interrupted, standing somewhere behind Britt.

My God, where are my manners? "Yes, please! Sit." Feeling a bit awkward in her own skin and not completely in control of her limbs, she lunged forward to catch his free hand. Naturally, she missed and knocked into the one holding the glass of very red wine. Of course it spilled. All over his white golf shirt. "Oh, my gosh! I'm so sorry!" Not thinking, merely reacting, she reached forward and dabbed at the red stain with her hands. "That was such a nice shirt, too. I'll buy you a new one. I promise," she rambled.

Mary tapped at her shoulder and handed her a damp rag, and Britt started to work trying to clean the large mark from the middle of his chest. The feel of defined pecs and abs were not lost to her, even through the shirt's thick cotton, and even despite her self-conscious panic.

Andre caught her wrists and smiled, instantly stilling her frenzied motion. "It's okay. I have plenty more shirts. This one was old. I wear it when I'm working around the house. Honest."

"If that's what you wear to work around your house, I'd love to see what you wear to go out to dinner," she mumbled, not intending for him to hear.

"I'd like that, too."

She jerked her hands away and cupped them over her mouth, rag and all. "Oh, God! I didn't think you'd hear that." Dropping them and wringing the rag like she wished she could wring her own neck, she stammered, "I've been drinking wine. I can't be held responsible for what comes out of my mouth."

He pulled on his shirt, which had begun to adhere to his chest and stomach like a second skin—which she appreciated—and smiled.

"Come to think of it, I can't control my hands very well after a couple of glasses, either."

"I'm not complaining." He winked. "I don't know many guys who would object to a beautiful woman with out-of-control hands."

Oh my God! He's flirting with me! She shivered as his white-hot gaze slid down her body, then slowly crept back up to her face.

"Okay, you two! You're killing me here." Mary sounded about as flustered as Britt felt but hid it well. She pulled Britt's arm, practically dragging her to the couch. "If you don't get your hands under control soon, I'll be forced to tie them."

When Andre's expression turned wicked-sexy, and sure she was going to melt into a puddle, Britt forced herself to look away. A few naughty comebacks shot to her mind, but she forced herself to remain mute. It was a lot safer that way. She had a feeling Andre played in a whole different league from her—in more ways than one—and although she was more than a little intrigued, she was also a tiny bit intimidated.

Mary eased the tension by shoving the nearly forgotten cardboard box in her hands. "Here. I'm dying."

Me too, but not for the same reason.

"Will you finally open this?"

"Gladly." Britt fought through the packing tape and pulled a smaller box out of the plain brown one. This one was emblazoned with, among other things, the words "Private Games" across the top. "What is this?" She read the top then the sides. "Some kind of board game? Why would my mother buy me this?"

"Haven't you heard of it? It's all the rage. It's a..." Mary cleared her throat. "...well, kind of a dating game. I read about it on the 'net. Your mom and I thought it would be the perfect gift."

"Oh, really?" Britt tried not to sound too insulted. "What do I need a dating game for? I'm doing just fine, thank you." Utterly embarrassed, she refused to look in Andre's direction.

"Oh, quit being such a spoilsport! I know you better than that. Let's have a look." Mary pulled the box out of Britt's hands and lifted the top off. "Let's pull a card."

"How about we don't?" Britt suggested, catching Mary's suddenly busy hands. She motioned with her eyes toward Andre.

"Oh. Yeah. Right." Mary set the game on the coffee table and dropped her hands back in her lap. "It was a silly idea. I confess." She gave an exaggerated sigh. "My love life is in the pits and I wanted the game for myself."

Britt hazarded a look at Andre, not surprised to catch him grinning with disbelief. To his credit, he kept his thoughts to himself.

He drained the rest of his glass and made a good show out of stretching and yawning. "Well, ladies, thanks for the nightcap. I think I'll head home now and hit the hay early. Tomorrow, I'm rebuilding the front porch on the old homestead. Want to get started early, since we're supposed to get some rain later." He stood and smiled down at Britt, staring hungrily at her cleavage. "Thanks again for the wine, and the fun." He leaned lower and his tongue darted out, moistening his lips. "Happy birthday, Britt."

This is it! By God, he is going to kiss me! She wetted her lips, closed her eyes, and waited, breathless.

A chaste kiss warmed her cheek.

What was that? The guy practically ravages me visually, kills me with those eyes, and then gives me a peck on the cheek? "Goodnight, Andre," she forced out, following him to the front door. "Thanks for bringing over my gift."

"No problem. See you later." He left.

Mary and Britt stared at each other for a moment then Britt shrugged as she shut the front door and returned to the living room. "Was he a bundle of confusing signals, or what?"

"No, I think his interest in you was obnoxiously obvious."

"Yeah, but at the same time it wasn't. I got mixed signals. He must be a player, giving me those kinds of crazy signals to string me along," Britt thought aloud.

"He's a sexy one, that's for sure. And there's a little hint of something in his eyes."

"You saw that, too?"

"Yeah. A touch of Bad Boy." Mary sat forward and picked up the game again, sifting through its contents. "For the heck of it, what about pulling one of these cards?"

Britt dropped onto the couch. "Did you really think this game was a good idea?"

"Naw, but I could tell when she called me that your mother's mind was made up. You know how she is. Although I admit, now that it's here, it does sound intriguing. It might be fun."

Britt considered Mary's suggestion for a moment. Fun—in any form—was one of her favorite things in world. She'd never backed down from a challenge. Skydiving, white water rafting, bungee jumping, she'd eagerly tackled them all, and had a riot. "Okay. Shuffle the deck. I'll draw a card."

Mary grinned and held the cards in her upturned palm. "Already done. I knew you'd say that. Pick a good one."

"You didn't stack the deck, did you?" Britt teased, plucking the top card from the stack.

"Heck, no!"

Britt studied Mary's devious smile—the woman was guilty as hell!—and read the card. "Go to the nearest BDSM-themed dance club and get the name and phone number of a Dom," she read aloud. "What the heck kind of dating game is this?"

"We'll just call it *Extreme Dating,*" Mary said, laughing. She ran to her duffel bag and dropped it on the coffee table.

"What do you have in there? And where do you suggest we'll find a BDSM club? I can't imagine one anywhere near here. We're smack-dab in the middle of the Bible Belt. Heck, the raunchiest billboard we have along the highway is the one with the donkey."

"You'd be surprised." Mary pulled out a fistful of black leather and shoved it at Britt. "Here, this is for you."

"What is it?" Britt unfolded what looked like a miniscule dress made to fit a small child. "You're not suggesting I wear this, are you? And how do you know about these places and I don't?"

"I have my sources." Mary fluttered her eyelashes and held a racy red leather dress, nearly the same shade as her ponytailed hair, getup to her chest. "How do you think this'll look?" One hand reached up and pulled the ponytail holder out of her hair, and she shook it, letting it fall in shoulder-length waves. "They say redheads can't wear red, but I happen to think this looks fantastic. What do you think?"

"It looks great, I guess," Britt said, admittedly sidetracked. She wanted to hear more about the club. "So, fess up. Have you been there? What's it like?" Britt waited impatiently, watching

Mary pull out spiked leather wristbands, fishnet stockings and various other accoutrements and set them on the coffee table.

"I'm not telling. But if you'd hurry up and put that dress on, you could go find out for yourself!"

Britt didn't need to hear another word. She raced to her room to dress.

Chapter Two

"Are you absolutely sure about this?" Not exactly trusting her friend, since Mary had driven them to what looked like an abandoned warehouse out in the middle of nowhere, Britt hesitated before getting out of the car. At this point, she wasn't sure which would be worse, Mary being right, or Mary being wrong and them both being jumped by a group of misguided teenagers out looking for a couple of lost women to mug.

For one thing, the *dress*—which hardly covered more than a bathing suit would—kept riding up her legs when she moved, the bottom of the skirt seeming to like resting right around her crotch. How in heaven's name would she dance—or even walk—without giving everyone in the place a free show? The rest of the outfit wasn't bad. The heavy silver jewelry was kind of sexy, and the stilt-like shoes made her legs look forever long.

Not good for walking on gravel though. She glanced out the window and grimaced.

"Yes, we're in the right place. Trust me." Mary climbed out of the car and waved for Britt to follow her.

She did. "You've been here before?"

"Yes."

"How did you find out about this place? It's in the middle of nowhere, looks like an abandoned warehouse—"

"I'm not telling. Suffice it to say, you don't know your best friend as well as you thought you did." Mary smiled over her shoulder, the expression clearly meant to jibe Britt.

Britt gritted her teeth against the comeback rearing up in her throat and smiled back as she stumbled across the gravel parking lot. When they approached the heavy steel door, Mary motioned for Britt to keep still then knocked in a short pattern.

The door opened, and a very tall guy in full gothic regalia—including multiple piercings on his face—opened the door, gave them both a once-over and motioned them inside.

"Wow, it's like 'Open Sesame'. Is there a code word too?" Britt murmured as she stepped inside the dark club. "Reminds me of a cave," she added after an initial sweeping glance. Dark, dingy, and echoey. Although this cave was packed full of people—mostly clad in black leather. Strange music played softly in the distance.

"You might want to get a drink before we go inside. It'll help you relax," Mary suggested.

"Why would I need to relax? I'm fine." She rolled her head from side to side. "See? As relaxed as can be."

"Just try to keep an open mind, okay? This is the lounge-slash-bar area. In the next room are the *other* parts."

"Other parts?" Now, she was curious. "What kind of parts? Body parts? Car parts?"

"Wine first." Mary pulled her to the bar and ordered them both a glass of red wine.

Britt sat on a barstool, swiveling around to check out the crowd. All types of people milled about, mostly young, mostly attractive, mostly dressed in black. Some wore collars and leashes and were led around the room by masked masters. Those—who she assumed were the submissives—were notably silent. The Doms—often men but not always—paused occasionally to speak with someone. "How do we find a Dom who'll talk to us? For some reason, I'm getting the impression this won't be easy."

"It might not be. Can't say I've tried to talk to one before. Sometimes, they'll come to you."

Suddenly nervous, imagining some masked, scary stranger approaching her, she swallowed half her wine. "What do I say if I'm not interested?"

"Thanks, but no thanks?" Mary suggested. "Seriously, it's all a game, and there are rules, but they're still just people inside that leather and latex."

A huge man wearing a leather mask and carrying a horse crop stomped by, his gaze cold and threatening.

"That's hard to remember." Britt looked away, hoping he wouldn't think anything of her staring, and finished off the rest of the wine. Within minutes, she felt braver, thanks no doubt to the alcohol. "Okay. I'm ready. Are you going to give me a rundown of the rules so I don't do something stupid?"

"Sure. I don't know everything, but this is what I've been told. Don't talk to the subs unless they speak to you. Keep quiet, don't interrupt the play. No catcalls or cheering. Keep your distance from the Dom's tools. Don't touch anyone's equipment—"

"As in genitals?"

"As in cat-o'-nine-tails."

"Gotcha. What else?"

"No pictures. And once you leave here, you don't know any of these people. They all have lives, families, jobs. What happens here, stays here. Oh, and since we've drunk alcohol, we cannot play." Mary hesitated at a pair of double doors.

"Really? Why's that? Er, not that I was planning on playing. At least, not the first time."

"It's not safe."

"Oh." A lump formed in her throat.

"Ready?"

She swallowed hard. "Yeah." For a split second, Britt tried to prepare herself for what she'd see, but having no idea of what to expect, she couldn't.

The doors opened, and a strange world opened with them. A dark world, with people in small fenced-in areas playing out their most secret fantasies in the middle of a small but milling crowd. As they walked past one "stage" after another, she became both more uncomfortable and more intrigued. The good news, the position of her dress was much less of a concern.

Then a familiar voice, male, smooth, sexy, made her turn around. *It can't be…* She scanned the crowd for Andre's face but didn't see it. *Strange coincidence. I could have sworn I heard his voice.* "Mary, did you hear Andre's voice, or am I hearing things?"

"Nope," she whispered, motioning for Britt to lower her voice.

"Wishful thinking, I guess." She turned back around to watch the scene in front of them. A tall, muscular Dom was demanding a woman clean his shoes. With her tongue. "Ewww." The Dom glanced at her, and she clapped her hand over her mouth and whispered, "Sorry."

"Would you please be quiet?" Mary whispered.

"Sorry, but that's gross. Why does she have to lick his shoes?"

"It's a submissive's role to do whatever pleases her Dom," a male's deep voice whispered in her ear, sending shivers down her spine.

"I…see…" She turned her head to see who the speaker was. *Andre! It had been him! I'm not losing my mind! What a relief. My medical coverage doesn't pay squat for mental health care.* "Andre? Fancy bumping into you here, of all places."

"Hi. Yeah, I had a change of plans. The weather forecast calls for rain all night. I won't be able to work on the porch tomorrow and a friend called me…" Dressed in the same fashion as everyone else, including tight leather pants that hugged a huge bulge front and center and a net shirt that gave her a glimpse of the muscles she'd only caught a touch of earlier—along with a pair of pierced nipples—Andre appeared to fit right in with the rest of the crowd. His gaze dropped to her breasts then climbed steadily lower. "Nice dress."

"Thanks." She tugged the hem back down her thighs. "Leather is tricky to wear." *Does wonders for you though.* Her gaze dropped to his crotch. *Please, tell me that's real.*

"You're doing fine. What do you think of this place? First time, I'm guessing."

"Is it that obvious?" She felt her face heating and wished she hadn't guzzled that glass of wine.

"Yeah, but that's okay. It's hard to hide."

"So, you've come here before?"

"Yeah." A passing woman—a beautiful blonde with long hair and a perfect body sheathed in black latex—tapped him on the shoulder and gave him a coy smile, and he gave her a slight nod in response. "This place is okay."

Who was that? His girlfriend? A sex partner—or whatever they call them here? What were the rules again? What am I doing? I don't belong here. For the first time since stepping foot in the bar, Britt felt completely out of place. She wanted to ask who the woman was, but couldn't. It wasn't her right. After all, she couldn't even call Andre a friend, yet. "I've seen a lot of things I've never seen before, that's for sure."

He chuckled, and the sound—plus his playful smile—pushed aside some of her former discomfort. "I bet you have. The first time's a real eye-opener. At least you came dressed. First time I stumbled into this place, I had on a golf shirt and khakis. I stood out like an Eskimo at a nudist colony."

She shared a soft laugh with him, enjoying the way his eyes sparkled when he smiled and noting the return of the hint of bad boy she'd seen earlier. At least now, she knew where that was coming from. "Are you by any chance a Dom?"

His eyebrows rose at least an inch. "Why do you ask?"

Because I wouldn't mind serving you, you sexy hunk of man. If you aren't already taken. "Well, you remember my birthday gift? The game? Um, we drew a Challenge card. We have to collect the name and phone number of a Dom."

"I'm not your traditional, professional Dom, no. So, I'm afraid you're outta luck. Sorry."

Darn! I mean, yea! I mean…oh, what do I mean? "Traditional? Is there such a thing? And professional? Are you telling me these guys are paid to get their shoes licked clean? What a deal! Where do I sign up to be a dominatrix? I have a few pairs of pumps that could use a good spit-shine." *Although being tied up, maybe teased with a little whippy thingy looks like fun.*

"There's a lot more to being a Dom than what you see. Besides," he leaned closer and whispered, "I think you'd rather do the licking, wouldn't you?"

She felt her eyeballs bugging from her head as the image of her kneeling at his feet, her fist gripping his huge cock and her tongue swirling round and round it like a lollipop shot through her mind. Her pussy tingled.

"Wouldn't you like to serve your master and receive great rewards in return?"

More tingles skittered up her spine. *Rewards. Wonder what kind he has in mind?* She imagined him knocking her flat on her back, parting her legs wide and pushing his cock deep inside her pussy. A lump completely closed off her throat.

"You've always wanted to be tied up, haven't you? Forced by a dark stranger."

How did you know?

"You know," His fingertip traced the line of her throat then continued lower and stopping just above her exposed cleavage, "the beauty of being a sub is in both the giving and in the receiving." His other hand cupped her chin and lifted it, and her gaze snapped to his eyes and froze there for a moment before sliding south to rest on his broad, smooth chest. She swore she could see his heartbeat pounding below the thick muscles. "When you please your master, you receive pleasure beyond your wildest dreams. Let me guess…" When he didn't continue, she glanced up. His smile was more wicked now than she'd ever seen it, yet she was tempted to press in closer to him rather than back away. He licked his lips then continued, "You like to be bent over and fucked from behind, right? That way, you can touch yourself and come over and over."

A sudden case of dizziness left her staggering and wobbly kneed. She gripped his upper arms and stared up into his eyes, eager to see if he was simply teasing her, or making some kind of offer. She couldn't speak. Her tongue was frozen to the roof of her mouth, and her mind had become lost in a hazy fog.

He released her chin and dropped his other hand from her chest. "Have you ever let a lover take complete control? Let him push you to your threshold then pull you back, over and over until you couldn't take it anymore?" While he didn't touch her, he stood so near she could feel the soft puff of air caressing her neck as he spoke. And heat radiated from his body.

"No." *But it sounds damn promising at the moment.* Some of the heat seemed to soak into her pores and shoot down to her pussy.

"Would you like to?"

Are you offering what I think you are? "Maybe." She felt the chill of wetness puddle in her panties.

He pulled a card from his pocket and handed it to her. "Call me tomorrow."

She glanced down and blinked away the blur of confusion and desire.

It was a regular card, from his work. Andre Cruz-Romero, Engineering Manager. She wasn't sure what she'd expected. *Andre Romero, Dom. Specializing in erotic torture.* "Okay."

"And wear the dress. I'll supply the rest. See you tomorrow night. I'm looking forward to it."

The tone in his voice as he said the last sentence left her breathless, speechless and both shivering and hot at the same time. Glancing around, she looked for Mary. She'd had enough teasing for one night. She needed to pay a visit with her friendly vibrator. Now.

Chapter Three

"I knew it!" Mary smiled triumphantly. Back at Britt's place, she gathered her things from the coffee table and couch and stuffed them in the duffle bag. "So, your hunky Andre's a Dom?"

"He's not my Andre. And he's not a Dom, at least not in the purest sense of the word, I guess."

"Whatever that means." Mary zipped her bag then slung it over her shoulder.

"My thoughts exactly."

"Sorry about abandoning you, by the way, but I figured you needed a little space. After the first sentence, I was squirming. I had to get outta there. Shit, that man can talk dirty. Is there anything he can't do?"

Not that I can tell. "I'm sure he has his shortcomings. All men do."

"True, but he seems to have a few more…uh…strengths than the average guy." Mary winked. "So, are you going to see him again?"

"Maybe. And it's okay you abandoned me. I found you, eventually," Britt said, stifling both a hint of jealousy over her friend's obvious lust over Andre and the truth about how pissed she'd gotten at the club. It had taken close to an hour to find Mary, huddled in the corner and talking to the scary giant with the whip. By the time she'd found her wandering friend, Britt had been downright seething.

Mary chuckled and winked. "At least I don't have to ask you if you had fun."

"I can't say I had fun—well, not an adrenaline-rush kind of fun—but I saw some interesting things there."

"Like Andre."

"He is the most interesting thing, er person, yes."

"I don't blame you. I'd kill to be tied up and fucked by that man."

And I'd kill you if you did! He's not mine yet, but if I get my way he will be soon. More jealousy wound up her spine. "He gave me his number. So, I guess I'm going on a date with him tomorrow night. Um, that is what it's called, isn't it? A date?"

"Are you playing in his dungeon or going out?"

His dungeon? Not a bedroom? "I'm not sure. I guess I won't know until I call him. He did ask me to wear this dress again, so can I borrow it for a couple more days? I'll have it cleaned before I give it back."

"Sure!" Mary gave her a gentle tap on the shoulder. "Look at you! Getting ready for your first time with a Dom. Are you nervous?"

Hell yes! "A little. Want to give me any pointers? Um, assuming you know about these things."

"To tell you the truth, I'm a watcher, not a doer. But I've learned one thing. Make sure you have a safe word so if he gets too carried away you can make him stop."

"Okay."

"Pick something easy to remember and pronounce, too. You wouldn't want to stumble over the word in the midst of some tense moment." Mary grinned. "That's about it." She shrugged then strolled toward the front door, and Britt followed her. "Good luck tomorrow. Have fun. And call me afterward. I want to hear all about it—um, some of the juicier parts, at least."

"Okay."

Britt closed the door and headed for bed, sure she wouldn't get a decent minute's sleep. Even after more than an hour since she'd talked to Andre, she was still a tingly, horny mess.

Thankful for the vibrator she had purchased on a whim but hadn't put to use yet, she rummaged through her dresser drawer and pulled it out.

She might be alone in body, but she had one hell of an imagination. She wouldn't be alone in her mind. After pulling off her dress and putting on some soft music, she lay on the bed, parted her legs and turned on the toy.

It hummed softly in her hand as she closed her eyes and imagined Andre's flirty, wicked smile. Her pussy immediately clenched around its own emptiness.

His words echoed in her ears, *Have you ever let a lover take complete control? Let him push you to your threshold then pull you back, over and over until you couldn't take it anymore? No doubt about it, tomorrow would be an experience she wouldn't ever forget.*

Her body already tense with anticipation, she parted her labia and rested the vibrator on her clit. Immediately with the first touch, heat rocketed through her body and she sighed. It wouldn't take much to make her climax at this rate.

The beauty of being a sub is in both the giving and in the receiving. When you please your master, you receive pleasure beyond your wildest dreams.

She slid the vibrator lower and pushed it inside, gasping at the intense sensations throbbing through her body. Every muscle from head to toe knotting tightly, she pulled it out then plunged it inside over and over, while she stroked her clit with her other hand.

You like to be bent over and fucked from behind, right? That way, you can touch yourself and come over and over.

She imagined herself lying in bed, her legs tied wide, Andre standing over her, watching. Her pussy tightened around the vibrator and her fingers teased her clit then pushed inside her ass. In her head, he smiled, cooing appreciative compliments about her ass and pussy. Encouraging her to come for him.

And she came, calling out his name into the darkness. Her body spasmed, her pussy rhythmically milking the vibrator, her anus pulsing around her finger until she had no energy left. Satiated, she slid the vibrator out, turned it off and set it on the nightstand.

And she slipped into a dream, where she and Andre fucked over and over and over.

*****

Andre made one last attempt to fix his unruly hair. It was humid outside, and he stood little chance of taming the curls. Extra gel did little good, and he didn't like making his hair stiff. Of all days, today he wanted it silky, touchable.

This was it. His dream come true.

Ever since he'd laid eyes on Britt Olson he'd wanted her. She was absolutely stunning, a classic northern-European beauty. Slim, delicately built with smooth ivory skin, pale blue eyes, naturally blonde hair and feminine features. There was an air of innocence about her, yet boldness, too. Strength, but also vulnerability. Intelligence, but also approachability. He had the feeling she didn't always speak her mind, and he yearned to know what secrets she kept hidden away in the cool depth of her soul. Like a deep pool, the surface seemed calm, but he wondered what currents churned below.

He wondered what a game of bondage and submission might bring to the surface. In fact, he ached to find out.

It hadn't been easy explaining to friends and family members why he'd bought the run-down farmhouse a couple of months ago when he could afford a much nicer home. The truth, he knew, would be too ridiculous for anyone to believe.

He had bought it for her. A stranger, yes, but a woman he'd felt an instant connection with. He sensed she felt the same. If things went his way, someday they'd live in the house together, work side-by-side fixing it up. Raise their children.

But one thing at a time. Tonight was an important beginning, and he wouldn't blow it. He'd make sure that by the end of the night, she'd be aching to come back for more.

Years of experience had taught him what most women wanted. They wanted a strong man who could be vulnerable at the right time. They wanted a man who could make demands, take control, but also give back more than he received. They wanted a man who would listen to them when they needed to vent without shoving solutions down their throats.

He could be all those things for her, and more.

After giving up on his hair, he went outside, climbed into his car, and drove to her home. His body was tense with expectation, his cock already at full staff before he'd gotten within a couple miles of her home. Memories alone stirred him to aching arousal. He parked, adjusted his pants to try to hide the telltale bulge. Finally accepting it was futile, he walked to the door. She'd know exactly how thrilled he was to see her. That wouldn't be such a bad thing. Nervous, he knocked and waited.

She smiled as she opened the door, and the sight of her nearly drove him mad with desire. As requested, she wore the skimpy black leather dress she'd had on last night. The dark leather was a striking contrast to her pale skin and hair. And the deep plunging neckline showed off delectable cleavage that he ached to explore with fingers and tongue.

"Hi," she cooed.

"Ready?"

"I'm starving. Dinner first?"

"Absolutely." He motioned for her to walk ahead of him.

The extra-short skirt showed off her long, slim legs to perfection, and hugged her surprisingly round ass, he noted as she turned to close the front door then brushed past him toward the car.

Licking his lips and wishing he were licking that ass, he followed her, shut her car door, then went around to the driver's side and took his seat. "We can do one of two things, and I'll leave it up to you. I have no preference." He glanced her way, and immediately doubted his ability to concentrate on driving. "I don't want to look like a cheapskate, but I'd like some privacy. So, either we can go get something takeout from a nice restaurant and go back to the house and eat, or we can go inside and eat at the restaurant of your choice. You decide."

She chuckled. "You made that decision easy by asking me to wear this. I might not mind being dressed like this at a BDSM nightclub, but I wouldn't want to wear it at a five-star restaurant."

He nearly slapped himself upside his head. "I should have thought of that. I swear it was an honest oversight. Would you rather go inside and change? You can bring that along for later."

Her cheeks turned a sexy shade of pink and his balls tightened. He couldn't wait to see more of that flush on her neck, chest…lower…

"Oh, that's okay. I vote for carryout. How about steak?"

"Sounds perfect. I'm always game for a nice rare hunk of meat."

"Me, too."

He peered her way and caught a playful smile. His drawers grew instantly snug, and he thanked whatever god was responsible for the blessing sitting next to him. Then he pulled out of her driveway, and chattering about nothing and everything, drove to the steakhouse. After parking, calling in the order from his cell phone, he shifted his body to face her.

It would be so easy to give in to the other hunger. The one that wasn't housed in his stomach. The one that was scorching him from the inside out. No doubt about it, tonight would be sheer torture—good torture, but extremely uncomfortable nonetheless.

The coy smile had vanished from Britt's face, replaced by a shy, nervous one. "This is so awkward."

"Just be yourself, Britt. No need to be nervous." He reached for her hand and gave it a gentle squeeze. "Tonight I just want to focus on getting to know you."

Relief softened her formerly tense expression and her eyes widened, making her look so painfully innocent and trusting he wanted to wrap his arms around her and pull her to him. "Really?"

"Did you assume we'd skip the beginning part and just go for the other stuff?"

She lifted her free hand and pulled at a lock of hair fluttering across her face on a breeze. She tucked it behind her ear. "Honestly, I didn't know what to expect. We didn't really talk about it last night."

"My fault. I should have been more specific."

"It's not that big of a deal. I know now, so we can go from here and just see what happens."

"Good." *I know what I'd like to happen. "So, why don't you tell me more about yourself. Thanks to the closing paperwork, I know a few basic facts about you, but I'd like to know more."*

"Like what?" Pulling at the hem of her skirt, she crossed her legs. Her thighs were trim and firm. Absolutely perfect. His palm itched to slide over the satiny skin.

"Like do you work out? You look very fit."

"I do, but not as often as I should. Maybe a couple of times a week. In between, I try to watch what I eat. Follow my own version of the low-carb diet."

Whatever you're doing, it's working. "You will eat tonight, won't you?"

"Oh! Absolutely!" She smiled and he suppressed a sigh. Her eyes glittered like diamonds. Her whole face lit up. She was a glorious sight. "I never let a good steak dinner go to waste. Meat, potatoes, bread. I won't leave a bit of it for the dogs."

"Good. I like to see a woman who's not afraid to eat in front of a man. No need to pretend. I want you to be yourself."

"In that case, how about ordering some dessert, too? I love that brownie-ice cream thingy they make here. It's sinful."

Sinful, like you are in that dress. "Glad to." Sporting a huge hard-on, and not wanting to walk into the restaurant and show everyone what he had on his mind, he called in the dessert order with his cell phone.

Seconds later, a waitress carted a large brown bag out to their car, handed it to Andre through the car window, and returned inside with Andre's cash payment tucked in her apron pocket. Andre, drooling both because of the scent of the food and the sight of the gorgeous woman sitting beside him, drove the few miles to his place. Then he parked, grabbed the bag, opened Britt's car door and ushered her to his front door, his gaze straying to her ass every chance it could. He tripped over a porch step and bumped into her back, and he had to fight the urge to drop the food, grab her body and press her firmly against him.

But he didn't do it.

Proud of himself for maintaining control, he reached around her, slid the key into the lock and opened the door.

She stepped inside and glanced around the living room. "You painted. It looks very nice. And the wood floors. Wow! Did you install new ones?"

"Oh no, these are the original floors. I sanded and refinished them."

"Really? I'd never have thought they could look this great." She smiled up at him and he returned the warm expression with one of his own.

He carried the bag to the dining room and set it on the table. "I'm glad you approve. I have a lot of plans for this house," he added honestly while not going into detail about what kind of plans he was referring to. It was much too soon to tell her all that he wished for the home—including who would inhabit it.

"You've done so much already. More than I did owning it for six years. My poor grandfather. It was too much for him to handle the last few years he and my grandmother lived here. But I have no excuse really. It sounds silly, but I didn't want to fix it up until after they were gone. I felt guilty. Like I was somehow hurting them by updating."

"It's different for me. You have memories tied to this place. I don't. Plus, I have friends in the trades who owe me favors." He walked into the kitchen for plates, glasses and other necessities.

"My gosh! Look at this kitchen. Is this the same house?" Britt exclaimed from behind him as she halted in the doorway. "It's…wow…like a showroom."

"You aren't upset, are you?" His hands full, he turned to face her, embarrassed by the obvious appreciation—nearing awe—he found on her face. "Well, I didn't do it by myself. Like I said, I have some extremely skilled friends."

"Are you kidding? No, I'm not upset. It's gorgeous. Are those cabinets solid cherry?" She stepped inside and softly stroked a door, and he nearly wilted as he imagined her touching him like that.

"Yep."

"And is this a real granite counter?" Her hand dropped to the cool, smooth stone counter. Her tongue darted out, moistening her lips as her hand ran over the counter's surface in long, slow strokes.

Gimme some ice. I'm in meltdown! "It is. My buddy works at a stone yard. So you like it? Be honest."

She took the glasses and wine from him and returned to the dining room, setting them on the dining table. "Very much. Believe me, I had no emotional attachment to the laminated stock cabinets and cheap plastic counters I put in. Yes, I'm very impressed by what you've done so far. I just wish I could have done as well."

He followed her on wobbly legs. "You did the best you could. Don't beat yourself up over it. This place wouldn't look like this if I didn't have friends to help. If I'd had to pay retail and labor for all this stuff, I'd have never been able to afford it," he lied. The last thing he wanted her to feel was guilt for not being able to afford the latest and greatest just because he could.

"Can I borrow those friends of yours sometime? My new place isn't in a shambles, but there are a few projects I wanted to tackle."

You won't be needing to do them if I get my way. And there's no chance I'm letting any of my beer-swilling buddies near you. They're animals. "Sure! What do you need? I'm fairly handy when it comes to small projects. I have my own Dewalt, too."

She giggled, the sound so charming and erotic, he wanted to say something silly just to hear it again. "Oh, yeah. That."

He handed her a plate and silverware and then pulled out the foam packages from the restaurant's paper bag. He put the dessert in the freezer for safekeeping then set one large container next to her plate. "A guy would have to be nuts not to appreciate a woman with her own power tools."

Clearly fighting another blush but losing the battle, she rolled her eyes. "I shouldn't have bragged. I only use it to hang pictures, assemble furniture, stuff like that. I'm sure it's more power than I need."

He paused after flipping the top of his container open. "That depends on what kind of power you're talking about," shot out of his mouth before he could stop it. He loved the game of double entendre, and he suspected Britt would be better than average at keeping up with him. Her mind was razor-sharp.

Eager to see if she'd gotten his message, he glanced at her.

Yep. She had. Her wide-eyed, shocked semi-smile said it all.

Eager to hear her comeback, he swallowed an apology and went back to unpacking his steak and potato.

"I thought you liked to be the Dom," she said in a low, sexy voice that sent shudders up and down his spine. "I may not know anything about this bondage and submission stuff yet, but I thought the whole idea was for the sub to be powerless."

He cut up his potato and dabbed on some sour cream then added salt. "You see, that's where you're mistaken. The sub actually has plenty of power. Are you intrigued?" He lifted his gaze to her face.

"Yes."

"Later."

Her shoulders dropped. "You're a tease."

"I've been called worse." He took a bite of his steak. "How's your dinner?"

"Delicious. So tell me, how did you get into this bondage stuff?"

He swallowed. "There are different levels, from casual—like lovers who tie each other up on occasion—to serious, people whose lifestyles are fashioned around it. I tend toward the more casual side, although I have a decent collection of equipment for someone who isn't living it twenty-four, seven."

Her fork halted midair. "Really? Will you show me?"

"Later. You're impatient, aren't you?"

"Yes, that's one of my biggest weaknesses. Very impatient."

"Interesting." He imagined the games he could play to take full advantage of her admitted shortfall and his cock swelled even more.

"What about you? I hate to admit a deep, dark, dirty secret and not know one about you."

"That was deep and dark? I think you could do better than that."

"Well, it's all you're getting for now. Your turn."

"Hmmm… I don't think you're ready to hear about the darkest, dirtiest…yet."

"Chicken," she teased, parting her lips and sliding a piece of meat into her mouth. They closed over the fork, the corners lifting into a flirty smile.

"Oh, no. I'm no chicken. Just don't want to scare you off."

She pulled the fork out and chewed, her gaze fixed to his. He enjoyed the way she looked in his eyes. Confident, attentive. "You haven't scared me off yet. What could be so bad?"

"Nothing. As far as weaknesses go, I'd say I tend to be very stubborn. Once I make my mind up on something, it's practically impossible to change it."

She nodded and took another bite of her steak, chewing and swallowing before saying, "I'm beginning to see that."

"What else do you see?"

"A man who knows what he wants and goes for it. You saw my house once and we closed only a couple weeks later. I've never seen a real estate transaction go that quickly." She paused a moment and her eyebrows dropped. "And I think you're a man with a lot of secrets."

"Me? No. I'm a what-you-see-is-what-you-get kind of guy."

She chuckled. "Liar." Leaning back and setting her fork and knife on her plate, she added, "I've had enough of this steak. It was delicious."

He glanced down at her dish. "You've only eaten a couple of bites."

"Want to save room for dessert."

"Fair enough. Do you want to take this home?" He stood and lifted both their plates.

"Sure. Thanks."

"Be right back." He wrapped their dinners and put them in the refrigerator then brought out the ice cream along with one spoon. He didn't miss her gaze as it locked on his hands.

"Only one spoon? You aren't going to make me eat that whole thing, are you?"

"No way." He set the dessert in front of her then carried his chair around the table and set it next to hers. "We'll share. I'll feed you." He lifted the spoon, scooped a bit of the white fluffy whipped cream off the side and put it in front of her mouth, breathlessly watching it open and close around the utensil. A tiny bit of white clung to her lip until she licked it away.

"Mmmm..." She closed her eyes, visibly relishing the taste. "So sweet and creamy."

Setting down the spoon, he plucked the cherry off the top, holding it by the stem, and ran it along the seam of her lips. They opened and her tongue slid out and swirled around and around. His heartbeat flew into double time and his cock throbbed.

Then she drew the cherry into her mouth slowly and opened her eyes. "I love cherries."

"So do I." He gave the stem a sharp tug until it pulled from the fruit trapped behind her teeth and dropped it on the table.

"Let me share." She leaned closer and pressed her mouth against his. He slipped his tongue out to taste her closed lips and then she opened them and sucked his tongue into her mouth, welcoming it into the sweet depth.

He found the cherry and drew it into his mouth, biting down to release a flood of sweet juices before opening to welcome her tongue inside. He moaned as her tongue stroked his, slowly swirling. His eyelids grew heavy. His balls grew tight. His heartbeat pounded in his head.

The taste of cherries, the soft scent of perfume, and the sound of her breathing intoxicated him. Quickly, his defenses crumbled, and he reached forward, his hands gripping the soft flesh of her breasts under her snug leather dress. A fingertip slid over the leather, catching the feel of a taut nipple lying below it.

She moaned in his mouth, the sound urging him on. One hand found the deep slitted V of her dress and slid inside. No bra! Still kissing her, he groaned at the feel of soft skin under his palm and eagerly sought her nipple. When he found it, he pinched it between his thumb and forefinger, and her mouth still working over his, she gasped and finally broke the kiss to drop her head back and expose the long column of her neck.

"Oh, God," she whispered.

He traced the line of muscle and tendon down her neck with his tongue, then nibbled where the collarbone met the neck, and she shrugged her shoulders and giggled.

"That tickles. I'm getting goose bumps."

"Good." He pinched her nipple harder and she gasped.

"Oh!"

"Do you like that?" He rolled it again between his finger and thumb. "A little bit of pain, a lot of pleasure."

"Yes," she said breathlessly, pushing her chest toward him. "More."

His tongue trailed lower between the crest of her breasts before he pulled the leather aside to expose the nipple he'd been teasing. Deep pink, erect, it beckoned him, but he resisted the urge to taste it. Instead he blew a soft stream of air on it and fought for control of his raging urge to fuck. "Your breasts are absolutely perfect." Then he felt her hand massaging his cock through his clothes, and his self-control snapped. Blind with need, he pulled her arms until she was sitting on his lap, her legs on either side of his hips. Her pussy ground into his cock, through layers of clothes, and he gritted his teeth, anxious for release.

He slid his hands around her back and dropped them to her ass, which had become conveniently exposed as her dress bunched up around her waist. She wore a thong. His fingers eagerly followed the line of velvet from her hips down between two firm, luscious ass cheeks.

Tense and frustrated because he couldn't allow himself the relief his entire body sought, he squeezed the flesh under his hands as his tongue drew circles round her pebbled nipple.

She moaned, the sound a sweet melody in his ears, as he pulled her nipple into his mouth and suckled. "Oh, yes!" she whispered, rocking her pelvis and grinding her pussy. "Oh, Andre. Yes. Fuck me."

Lifting one hand from her ass, he pushed her dress aside to expose her other breast, and took great care to give it as much attention as the first one received.

Her pleas continued, her voice rising until he knew he had to stop. He knew his limits, and he sensed she was nearing hers as well.

When he ceased, instead of drawing her to him in a warm hug, she pulled back, and looked at him, clearly confused.

"What's wrong?"

He sighed. It was never easy to explain these things to a woman. He hoped she'd understand.

Chapter Four

She was so close to orgasm she could practically taste it. He had to know what he was doing to her. What man stops things midway and then makes excuses? It made no sense. She was perfectly willing to go all the way.

She studied his flushed face for a clue but found none. So she waited.

"This probably sounds weird, but I think we should wait."

Is Andre a male? She'd never known one who turned down sex. "Why?" Suddenly uncomfortable, she scrambled to her feet, adjusted the top of her dress to hide her breasts and pulled down her skirt.

He watched her with a pained expression, convincing her he was as ready for sex as she was. So why stop? "Because it's too soon."

"Too soon for what? We both want to. Don't we?"

"Oh, yes." He nodded boyishly.

"You are certainly no virgin."

"No." He pulled her chair closer and motioned for her to sit.

She sat. "Neither am I."

"Glad to hear it."

He combed his fingers through his hair and she stifled a sigh. The man had amazing arms. An amazing body. She was dying to see what hid behind his snug short-sleeved shirt and trousers. But would he ever let her?

"I want to be honest about this. Forthright. We don't need to play games, do we?"

"Actually, dating and sex are both games, aren't they? Games of seduction. The chase is half the fun." She gazed into his eyes, hoping to find the truth. A notion struck her swiftly and without mercy. She glanced down. *I'm making this too easy for him!* "Ah. I see. So, are you one of those guys who get bored if it's too easy to get the girl?"

"No. But I'm a guy who likes to savor every moment, from the first time you look in each other's eyes..." He leaned forward and his heated gaze captured hers, making her breathless and squirmy. "...to climax. Why rush things? We have all the time in the world."

She fought to speak. Her tongue felt thick and clumsy. "Um...I guess it's that impatience thing again."

He smiled and her pussy tingled. "Oh, yes. We'll be exercising that little limitation of yours. I enjoy taking advantage of a woman's weaknesses, am not above using them for my own benefit."

"You jerk!" She reached out to give him a playful slap, but he caught her wrist and held it firmly, mid-strike.

He squeezed slightly and his expression grew intense, hot, pussy-melting. "You'll be grateful. I guarantee it." With a slow nod, he released her hand. "Domination and submission are about more than spreaders and cat-o'-nine-tails. At its best, it's a powerful tool that can help a relationship strengthen on all levels."

She reflexively rubbed her wrist to return blood flow to her hand. "I don't follow."

"What are the most important elements of a relationship to you?"

Beautiful eyes. Look at that face! He's so hot. So intense. Oh, what did he say? Unable to concentrate when staring at his face, she dropped her gaze to her hands.

"What is important in a relationship," he repeated as if he'd read her mind.

"Um...trust, for one."

"Yes. And blindly putting your body in a man's hands, and allowing him to serve your every need, to push you to explore aspects of yourself you've never dared delve into. To open yourself up to another human being like you've never done before. Those all build a very intense relationship where trust is absolute. Wouldn't you like to know without a doubt how your man feels? How he thinks? What he needs? Wouldn't you enjoy being in a relationship where you're free to tell him your deepest desires and fears? Where you're free to explore and experiment however you like?"

"Yes." She looked up into his eyes. "I would."

"This is new to you. Trust me. We'll take it one step at a time."

She nodded, not sure exactly how she felt. "Okay. What's next? Can I see your equipment? Your dungeon?"

"Are you sure you're ready?"

"I'm, uh, curious. And nervous. Maybe if I saw it, I'd feel better. At least, then I'd know whether my imagination had run wild."

"Okay. We can save the dessert for later." Taking her hand in his, he stood and picked up the dish of ice cream. After covering the uneaten dessert and stowing it in the freezer, he led her across the kitchen to the basement stairs. "It's down here. Just remember. We will only do what you're ready for. One step at a time."

She felt her palm sweating as it pressed against his, and her heart hammered against her ribs as she descended the stairs she'd trotted down zillions of times in the past. Now, they didn't lead to her workout room and laundry facilities. Instead, they led to a strange new world, and she wasn't sure if she was ready to enter or not.

Trust. That was what it would test. How could she trust a man she'd spent such a short time with?

He paused at the foot of the stairs, at the door that had once led to her workout room. "Ready?"

"Yes. It's just stuff. Nothing to be scared of."

He smiled warmly and pushed open the door, and she pulled her gaze away from his handsome face to scan the room beyond.

The doorframe offered welcome support as she slowly took in the details of the room. "Wow. Those aren't weight benches and stair climbers in there, that's for sure."

All but one wall were painted black. The fourth was mirrored as it had been when she'd lived in the house. And strange contraptions filled much of the space. One looked like some kind of swing, another, a large box resembled a dog crate, and still others that looked like various racks for medieval torture. The room wasn't romantic—not in any sense—yet it stirred something deep inside. A slightly uncomfortable feeling that made her tingly and energized. Her pussy was dripping wet, both from Andre's earlier kisses and her curiosity of what was to come next. She'd never felt so much anticipation mixed with reluctance. It was a crazy brew that made her all jittery inside. "When do we start?"

"We already have. It's a process, Britt. Not an event."

Her gaze fixed on the swing, she nodded. "That one looks interesting. How do you get into that contraption?"

Her hand in his, he led her closer, then reached for one of two bands overhead, secured at opposite ends of a metal bar suspended from the ceiling. He fastened it around her wrist. "First we secure your arms like this." He buckled the second one around her other wrist, and she shuddered. The simple loss of control was already making her hot.

Andre stood in front of her, his hands sliding down her arms then skimming her sides. His thumbs tickled the sensitive flesh of her breasts. "Then you sit back." He dropped one hand, reaching behind her as he eased her back with the other one. Something bumped her spine. "This part rests at the small of your back and the other slides under your ass." He helped her into position then smiled. "Your thighs go into the stirrups."

Stirrups? White heat shot through her body as he first lifted one leg and secured it and then did the same to the other. His gaze dropped to her pussy, which was barely covered by the slim strap of her thong. Her breathing came in short gasps as her heart raced.

"Comfortable?" he asked. One hand gripped her ankle and the other traced a line from foot to knee.

She gasped. Her pussy flamed. *Not at all! Hot, bothered, and miserably horny is more like it.* Her blood heated to boiling and goose bumps followed in the wake of his touch. "Yes…"

His exploring fingers wandered higher, over the band of leather holding her thigh until it tickled the sensitive skin of her inner thigh. "How do you feel?"

So hot I could melt! She drew in a deep breath, catching a hint of an unfamiliar musky odor. "Uh, really good."

"Oh, you can do better than that." His fingers drew lazy circles on her inner thigh, each time venturing closer to her pussy. "How do you feel? What are you thinking?"

"Think? I can't think. Not when you're doing that." She tipped her head and motioned toward his hand.

He chuckled. "Do you want me to stop?"

Don't you dare! "Hell, no!"

He chuckled, his grin wicked. "What if I do this?" His fingertip traced the line of her thong.

I wouldn't complain. Her eyelids dropped closed and her whole body stiffened. "Oh, God."

He continued to stroke her pussy through the thin material. "How do you feel now?"

Is he a closet shrink? What's with all the questions about feelings? I don't want to talk. I don't want to think. I just want to fuck. "I…oh…" She couldn't speak. Her thigh muscles became rigid, pulling her legs further apart as she opened herself to his touch. "More."

"Hmm... Seems to me you're in no position to make demands," he teased. "I asked you a question. I expect an answer. How do you feel?"

Like stuffing a gag in your mouth, ripping your clothes off, and fucking you until you're as brain-dead as I am. "I can't."

"I can stop." He pulled his hand away.

"No!" She struggled with the bindings at her wrists. "Oh, please, don't stop."

"Answer my question, Britt," he demanded returning to caressing her pussy with long, slow strokes. "How do you feel?"

"Like I'm going to combust."

"What about up here?" He tapped her chest. "What do you feel in here?"

"A little tight. Could be cardiac arrhythmia, maybe."

He chuckled. "That's not what I meant. What do you feel in your heart and soul?"

So deep! It's impossible to meditate with my legs spread wide and his hand on my pussy. "Er...elation?"

"Is that a question or an answer?" One finger slipped inside her thong and teased her slick lips.

"Oh, God! How do you expect me to carry on a conversation like this?" She struggled to tip her hips up and take his finger deeper inside but she couldn't. The scent of her own arousal filled the air and her lips dried. She licked them.

"You must try. I want to know everything. What you're thinking, feeling, seeing, hearing, smelling."

"That I can handle. I see a sexy man driving me to the brink of insanity."

He chuckled again. "Well, that's a start. Tell me more."

Glad to see I'm amusing you. "I smell my own pussy's wetness."

"Heavenly, isn't it? I'm getting hot from your scent alone."

Then fuck me. She shuddered and her insides clenched tight.

"What else? What do you hear?"

"Your finger sliding in my juices and your sexy voice."

"This sound?" He moved his finger more vigorously, producing more of the erotic, soft sounds. "It's so sexy, makes me so hard I want to drive my cock deep inside you."

"Please do so. I wouldn't object."

"Nope. Not yet. Remember, I'm the one in control here. I demand. You do."

She groaned as he hooked his finger to stroke the sensitized walls of her vagina. "You're killing me here."

"You'll live. I promise." He pushed his finger deeper inside and she screamed in delight.

"Oh, yes!" Her hands gripped the cool steel bar above her head as she tried to leverage herself and push her pussy against his hand. It didn't work. She had no control over the depth of his penetration. She nearly wept in frustration, then consciously tightened her vaginal walls around his finger.

"That's it, love. Oh, yes, so tight." Andre pulled his finger out, then pushed two inside. "This is all you'll get today. But you will come for me to show your gratitude."

She was so close. Every muscle inside pulled into a cramped ball. Wave after wave of heat rushed through her body, but she couldn't release. Something was stopping her.

"Come for me, Britt."

"Believe me, I want to."

"Come." He plunged his fingers in and out in a slow, seductive rhythm.

The threshold seemed just beyond reach. She pulled deeper inside herself and tried, imagining his cock driving into her. But her imagination wasn't enough to push her over the edge. "I can't."

"You will." With his second hand he stroked her clit, drawing slow circles, round and round in time with the fingers thrusting in and out.

She felt herself losing control, felt her breathing speed up, her legs quivering, her stomach tightening. "Yes! Oh, yes."

"Are you coming?"

"Almost."

"Tell me." The pace of his plunges sped up and he increased the speed of his strokes over her clit as well. Each touch drew her closer. Each time his fingers filled her pussy, she flamed hotter. Each time she drew in a breath, she grew dizzier with need.

And then she felt the flush of impending climax, and she sighed, relieved, giddy, as the climax took over and her body spasmed, sweeping her away into a cloud of energy and light and pleasure. Each heartbeat pounded in her ear as she came, counting out the beat of time for what seemed like an eternity. And then she sagged, every part of her body relaxing. "Oh." Her eyelids lifted and she focused on Andre's face.

He gave her a warm smile, lifted his hands to his nose, inhaled and drew each finger into his mouth, sucking them like a lollipop. "Delicious."

Her face flamed.

"That's enough for one day." He unstrapped her thighs and helped her find her footing before releasing her wrists. "Did you enjoy?"

She stumbled slightly, catching her balance by gripping his upper arms. "Wasn't it obvious?"

"Anyone can come. An orgasm is rarely disappointing, but I want to know if you enjoyed it all—the swing, the shackles."

"It was very erotic. Yes, I liked it. A lot."

"Good! Just wait 'til you see what I have in store for you next time." He drew her into an embrace and touched his mouth to hers, and she tasted herself on his lips. "Next time, you'll show me exactly how much you appreciated it. Understand?"

She licked her lips and clung to him, relishing the feel of his hard planes as they pressed against her soft curves. His erection was a rigid bulge under his pants, pressing seductively against her lower stomach. "I will. I promise."

"Good. I can't wait. Tomorrow, then." He kissed her softly, his moist lips sliding over hers. And then he released her and she staggered, unsteady, dizzy and exhausted. He gripped her waist and held her until she was firmly on both feet and her wobbly legs were able to support her weight.

"Tomorrow?"

"Yep. I want to give you some time to prepare."

Prepare for what? "Okay."

"I'll take you home now. Did you bring a purse or anything?" He followed behind her as she slowly ascended the stairs.

"Yes. I nearly forgot." She went to the dining room for her purse.

He stopped in the kitchen and pulled a container out of the refrigerator. "And I want to make sure you take this. You might get hungry later." He winked.

Her stomach growled in response, and she salivated. "Oh, yes. I'm starving now."

Holding his hand, she walked out to the car, settled into her seat then, a smiling, giddy goof, she rode in silence, determined to be fully prepared for tomorrow—whatever that meant.

Maybe it was all a silly game, but she was hooked. Andre had already proven to be an attentive, masterful lover. And he hadn't even actually made love to her yet—in the purest sense of the word. She wanted to learn more, to overcome what reservations remained. To explore and grow and experiment.

And Andre was the perfect man to do that with. Perfectly handsome, gentle, sexy…and patient. The man had the self-control of a saint. But she was determined to find a way to shake that a bit. Next time, she wanted to see him as desperate for release as she was.

Chapter Five

A lengthy Internet field trip revealed some interesting pictures, but little else. She found lots of photographs of bondage gear. Spreaders and special toilets—yuck!—and ball gags, and leather straightjackets. All kinds of stuff. But nothing about the actual use of the items, or the Dom-submissive lifestyle. How would she be prepared if she didn't know what she was preparing for?

Finally, frustrated after hours of scouring the 'net, she called Mary. Since her friend lived only a few blocks away, she was at Britt's door within minutes.

"It's about time you called me!" Mary burst into the room with her usual bluster. "What happened last night? Give me all the juicy details."

"I'm not telling you anything. Come over here and help me."

"You promised." Mary plopped into the kitchen chair Britt had pulled up to the computer. "I can't believe you're holding out on me."

"There isn't much to tell."

"Much. Ha! You expect me to believe that? You went on a date with an incredibly sexy man, wearing a leather dress—my leather dress, may I remind you?—not to mention he's a confessed Dom. Either you think I'm completely ignorant, or you're hiding something."

"I'm not hiding anything. I just like to keep things private."

"Since when? You told me when you lost your virginity. I taught you how to perform oral sex on a guy. Remember that?"

"How could I forget?" Britt giggled, remembering the scene in Mary's parents' kitchen, Mary being caught by her obnoxious baby brother, Adam, as she was sucking and slurping on a carrot.

"Up until now, we've talked about everything." Mary's voice echoed the hurt and disappointment in her eyes. "We've been friends since kindergarten."

"And we're still friends. I love you like a sister." Britt gripped Mary's hand and gave it a squeeze. "I just don't know how to talk about this stuff. It's all so strange and new to me. I honestly don't know how I feel about any of it yet."

"Then why did you call me?"

"I wanted to do some research on the Internet, but I can't find anything. I was hoping you could help me."

That seemed to boost Mary's suddenly glum mood. "Okay. What are you looking for?"

"Stuff on the bondage lifestyle. I found lots of sites that sell bondage equipment, but nothing else."

"You're looking under the wrong key words. Scoot over." Mary settled her chair in front of the keyboard and punched in a command. A black page with dozens of links appeared. "See? Lots of stuff. You can find anything on the 'net if you know where to look."

Britt skimmed the headings. "Oh, this is great! Thanks!" She clicked on a link for slave training, and immediately felt a flush spread over her face.

"What is it?"

"This…this sounds like Andre. He kept talking about my thoughts and feelings. I didn't know what he was doing."

Mary's eyebrows lowered as she read the glaring white print on the black page. "Master and slave are a little different from sub and Dom, although the difference between them is subtle. A slave eventually grants her choices to her Master where a submissive doesn't. It sounds like Andre has big plans for you."

"Yeah, it does." She squirmed as she read the slave rules, all one hundred and twenty-eight of them. In one way, the idea of serving someone, of turning over her will and freedom to a Master was exciting. In another it was absolutely terrifying. "Do you think he'll expect me to follow all of these?"

"It says you can choose how to interpret these rules for yourself."

"It also says that eventually I'd have to make a choice to let him do all the decision-making for me. I can't imagine doing that."

"It's new. You have to go slow. He's not asking you to do them now, is he?"

"No. We just played around with a swing in his basement. It was an amazing experience."

Mary grinned. "I bet it was. But what do you think about all of this?"

"I'm not sure. But at least now I'm not going into it blindly. I wonder if that's what he meant." Britt skimmed further down the list of rules. "These rules include undressing in public, and licking his ass clean? Oh, God! Do I have to get my labia pierced?" She shuddered at the imagined pain.

"Sounds like you need to talk to Andre. Find out what he's thinking. Maybe he doesn't want to take it this far."

"I guess you're right."

"When are you seeing him again?"

"Tonight. And he said to come prepared." Britt clicked the print icon at the top of the screen. "At least I'll have this."

"Sounds like a good start." Mary stood and rested her hands on Britt's shoulders.

Her eyes drifting from one shocking rule to another, Britt muttered, "After reading it, though, I wonder if I'm really cut out for this. Look here. It says he will decide what my sexual orientation is. How can he do that? My undergrad psychology professor said we can't even make that choice for ourselves. I'm not a lesbian."

"Don't worry. I'm sure he'll take things slow for you. I've got to go. Call me if you need me."

Britt's gaze refused to stray from the screen. "Okay. Thanks for coming over so quickly. Really."

"No problem." Mary pulled open the front door and exited, leaving Britt with a horde of doubts and fears running through her mind. And a heaviness in her pussy.

She couldn't deny it. For some reason, although the idea of being Andre's slave was scary, it also made her hot and bothered—in a good sense.

What would tonight bring?

* * * * *

That night, after a full day's work, she sat in her living room waiting for Andre to arrive, barely able to contain her jitters. She squirmed. She paced. She chewed her lip. She played with her purse strap.

How would she ever get through the evening? She was a walking bundle of nerves. At one point, she even picked up the phone and dialed his cell phone number, intending to cancel. But before it rang, she hung up.

This was silly! Not once had he ever made an unreasonable demand—unless she counted his unusual request to chitchat while in the middle of heavy petting. He'd never told her she couldn't look him in the eye, or had to kneel on the floor with her head down, or had to have sex with another woman.

That website was for people who lived the extreme. Outside of the fact that Andre had a basement full of bondage gear, he didn't appear to be one of *those kind*.

Yes, everything would be fine. He was a sexy, kind man. They would have a great time together.

Her doorbell made her jump nearly out of her skin, highlighting the fact that her feeble attempts at calming her fears hadn't helped much. Determined to find out exactly what Andre's intentions were, she scooped up her purse and walked to the door.

When she opened it, she found Andre standing on the porch, a huge bouquet of red roses in his hand.

"Hi, beautiful." His gaze wandered over her face, and his wide smile faded as he handed her the flowers. "Are you okay?"

"Oh, yes. I'm fine." She took the bouquet and turned toward the kitchen to put it in water. "They're beautiful. Thanks."

Andre followed her. "You look gorgeous." He slipped an arm around her waist and pulled her closer then placed a chaste kiss on her cheek.

She felt herself flinching slightly.

"What's wrong?" he repeated, this time more sternly. He took her hands in his and coaxed her to face him. "Why won't you look me in the eye? What happened?"

"Nothing happened. I'm just nervous." She lifted her eyes, meeting his penetrating gaze.

"Why?"

"I read some things on the 'net."

"I see." He nodded. "Let's go talk." He took her hand and they walked outside, down the sidewalk and past his car.

"Where are we going?"

"On my way over I passed a nice park. It's a beautiful day."

"Okay." She strolled beside him, enjoying the feel of his warm hand wrapped around hers.

"I see you took my request to heart. I'm very pleased."

"I'm glad you're happy. Although I have to admit, reading that stuff has made me a little unsure about things," she confessed, knowing she had to be honest. There was no way she'd be able to pretend to enjoy some of those things on that list. Heck, some of them sounded downright excruciating and humiliating. She was an independent, intelligent woman.

Allowing another human being to treat her—or any woman for that matter—like trash went against everything she believed in. This was one instance where complete honesty was vital. He had to understand where she was coming from.

"But it has made you aware of what being submissive can mean. And it's opened you up. You're talking about things now instead of hiding."

"Sure, out of shock and fear."

He sighed. "If you feel that strongly about this, then maybe it isn't for you. That's okay. I was just hoping we'd be able to talk about it. No rules are set in stone. I…haven't done anything wrong, have I?"

She glanced at him, catching his forlorn expression. He looked genuinely disappointed, and that left her feeling worse. "No, you haven't. I'm just being goofy. Maybe a little defensive. I'm sorry. I do want to talk about it."

They rounded the corner and followed the path into the park. She pulled her snug skirt down over her bottom and sat on a swing, heating slightly at the memory of the last swing she'd sat on. He stood in front of her, his legs straddling her knees. His hands gripped the chains suspending the swing and his gaze fixed to hers. "Tell me. Please. What did you read?"

"I found this site about Masters and slaves. It had over one hundred rules. All sorts of things about piercing body parts, stripping naked in public, kneeling nude with eyes lowered, the Master choosing the slave's sexual orientation. Enemas and whipping and humiliation. Some of the milder stuff I could handle—as a bedroom game, maybe. I'm too independent, too stubborn, to live like a slave all the time. And I know for a fact I couldn't handle torture. Pain does nothing for me sexually. Some of those punishments were—do I need to explain further?"

"No. I understand. Really."

She hesitated and tried to read his expression. It hadn't changed. Was still encouraging and gentle and kind. Her heart felt heavy even though she was relieved. "Are you disappointed?"

"No way! I'm glad you told me. I'm glad you've opened up to me. That's all I ever wanted."

She felt a giggle wiggling up her throat. "Really?"

"Later, if or when you decide we should, we can go over those rules and talk about each one. Until then, we'll talk about other things. We can explore and learn about each other. I'm not just looking for a slave, Britt. I'm looking for my future wife. I want to settle down. Get married. Have children."

"You do? You are? I would never have—"

"Yeah, you figured I was out for a good time. Miss Right-for-Now. I'll ask you the same question. Are you disappointed?"

"No," she answered honestly. "I've been feeling the itch to settle down, too. It's time. My life is good. I'm not needy or desperate, so I know I'll make the right decision for the right reasons."

"I'm glad."

She didn't know what to say. It was mighty soon to be talking about marriage. In the past, if a guy mentioned marriage on the second date, she'd bolt. Rushing into a serious relationship was plain stupid.

But with Andre, in this situation, it felt right. She needed to know where he was headed, what he expected. Knowing he wanted more than a woman to chain to the wall eased her fears considerably. Knowing he understood her reservations, and supported her decisions, made her feel even better…cherished.

If Andre Cruz-Romero was everything he seemed to be, she could see herself falling fast and hard for him. Like a block of cement from a third-floor window. *Thunk.*

Then the image of the basement popped into her head. "I wonder, what will you tell your future kids about the toys in the basement?"

He grinned, stepped around her and gave her back a push, sending her swinging into the air. "That's Mommy and Daddy's playroom. My kids will be so spoiled they won't care what's down there."

She closed her eyes, enjoying the feeling of the fresh, cool air blowing in her face as she ascended and the funny feeling in her belly as she descended. "That's where you're wrong. Kids are like all humanity. They want what they can't have."

"Hmm. You probably have a point. Do you have any suggestions?"

"Keep the door locked?"

"Sounds like the perfect solution, at least until they're teenagers and learn how to pick a lock." He plopped into the swing next to hers and watched as she skidded her swing to a stop, sending a cloud of dust up from the ground. "Are you ready for some dinner? It's a work night. I don't want to keep you out too late."

She stood and took his hand in hers, giving it a playful squeeze. Her shoulder brushed against his arm and she felt her face warming with a blush. "Yes, I'm starving. Let's go eat." As they walked back to her place, she added—surprising herself, "Then, maybe we can go back to your place for a little while? I'm in the mood for a visit to the playroom. I've rediscovered a fondness for swings."

Chapter Six

After eating more than her share of jambalaya at an upscale seafood restaurant nearby, Britt eased into the passenger seat of Andre's racy red Mustang and smiled. "That was delicious. Thank you."

"You're welcome." He started the car and she watched him, intent to study his features as he drove.

She could look at his face forever, the hollows under his high cheekbones. The curve of his lips. The long eyelashes that fringed his eyes.

Sure, she'd had her moments of doubt about where to take the relationship. But deep down, she'd known he would be the sweet, gentle, sexy man she'd thought all along. Attentive, patient to a fault…and a genuine pro at seduction and flirting. By the end of dinner, Britt was not only laughing at his wit, but squirming, for an altogether different reason than she had been earlier.

And the silence that fell over them as he drove the short distance to his house did nothing to ease the burning between her legs, yet she didn't feel compelled to fill it with incessant, meaningless small talk to distract herself. Instead, she watched familiar neighborhoods pass by and imagined what game they might play that evening. Would he tie her up? Would he spank her? Would they make love?

Her instincts told her they would, and she was glad she'd made special preparations just in case. Every inch of her body was shaved smooth, including *down there*. Being completely shaved made her feel sexy. So did the lace thong and bra she wore under her skirt and top. She hoped Andre would appreciate the special preparations she'd made.

She knew it wouldn't be long before she found out. As they turned down his street, he reached across and slid his right hand up her thigh. Her pussy started throbbing instantly, and she shifted her posture slightly, parting her knees and tipping her hips up, giving him access to the more delicate regions under her clothing.

Unfortunately his straying hand couldn't stay where it was long enough. There were real drawbacks to manual transmissions.

She groaned when, just before his fingertips dipped under the hem of her skirt, he had to shift the car into second gear.

"What's wrong?" He slid her a playful smile.

"Oh, nothing," she said on a sigh.

"Put your hand on my stick."

"Your what?" She reached for his lap, figuring there was only one stick he had to be thinking of.

"That's not the one I had in mind, but I like the way you think." He winked then turned his attention back to driving as she rubbed the rigid swelling at the front of his khaki pants.

"Well, if you didn't mean this one, what stick were you talking about?"

"Here." He patted the gearshift, and she lifted her hand, raising it to her face to hide her heating cheeks.

"Oh! I can't believe I thought—sheesh! My mind's in the gutter."

"I'm not complaining."

"No, what guy would?" Encouraged by his smile, she dropped her hand to his lap again and began caressing his cock through his clothes, for which she received a gratifying groan of pleasure.

"You, my dear, are wicked." He sighed. "I like wicked."

She playfully patted the bump in his lap. "I can tell. I can't wait to get my hands on this."

He chuckled. "I can't wait either."

"And my mouth, and tongue." Feeling naughty, she licked her lips and continued stroking.

"Just wait until I get you inside, you little tease."

"Who's teasing?"

He pulled the car into his driveway and cut the engine then got out and opened her door for her before leading her up to the porch. "We'll find out in a moment who's teasing, won't we?"

"Now it's my turn to say I can't wait." She intentionally lowered her voice, erasing the playful tone. "But before we go in, I want to tell you something."

He turned the key in the front door's lock then faced her. "What is it?"

"I want to tell you again how much I've enjoyed today. The walk in the park, the dinner. But most importantly, the time you took to talk about my feelings. I don't think many men have the patience to do that. I…half expected you to say 'fine' and leave."

He shook his head, furrowed his eyebrows and rested his hands on her shoulders. "I'm more than a Dom. I'm a man first."

"I know."

"I was serious when I said I'm looking to settle down. It's too early to talk about this, I know. But I want to be honest with you. I won't pursue a relationship that I believe is bound to fail eventually." He paused, licked his lips and tipped his head a little closer. "And I won't ruin something that has the potential to be wonderful by pushing too hard."

"You think this could be wonderful?" she managed to squeak out. It wasn't easy speaking with her breath jammed up somewhere below her breastbone.

"Don't you?" He pressed his mouth against hers, and she nearly crumbled to the ground.

Her knees went limp, and she wrapped her arms around his neck to hold on as he slowly, deliciously explored her mouth with his tongue. His kiss was as patient and seductive as he was. Warm tingles washed down her neck and pooled between her legs, and she pressed her pelvis forward and ground her pussy into his leg. A soft moan sounded in her head.

He broke the kiss.

Dizzy, and having forgotten where she was, she opened her eyes.

"We better take this inside before it goes any further," he half-said, half-growled.

Unable to speak or think…or do much of anything requiring the coordination of multiple neuron pathways, she merely nodded.

He smiled, took her hand, and led her inside. "Do you need something to drink?"

Drink? Oh, yes! A big glass of wine would go a long way toward getting rid of the last nervous jitters, but probably not a good idea. She coughed into a cupped hand to clear her clogged throat. "Some water would be perfect."

"Coming up." He patted the couch as he passed it. "Make yourself comfortable. I'll be right back."

She glanced at the soft chenille fabric on the couch and carefully considered the many meanings of the words *make yourself comfortable*. So many possibilities. One could take them literally, change into sweats and recline on it like a couch potato. Or…one could take them another way…

Oh, what the hell? She pulled her skirt off and stepped out of it, taking care to leave on her high-heeled pumps. Then she pulled off her top and positioned herself in a sexy reclining pose and watched the doorway to the kitchen for Andre.

She wasn't disappointed by his reaction.

His jaw nearly dropped to his chest. But his shocked expression was quickly replaced by one that made her pussy wet with anticipation.

He smiled, licked his lips like a hungry lion, and took long, purposeful strides toward her. When he reached her side, she half expected him to pounce on top, but thankfully…or not so thankfully…he didn't.

Instead, he handed her the glass of cool iced water. "Your water." He visibly swallowed.

Feigning nonchalance, not easy when facing the heat of a raging inferno in his eyes, she took the glass from him and smiled. "Thank you." She sipped daintily before handing it back to him. "Very…er, refreshing."

He barely had the glass on the coffee table before he swept her into his arms and carried her down the hallway.

"Where are you taking me?" She giggled, feeling small and weightless in his strong arms. He carried her with such ease.

"To my bedroom." He pushed open the door, revealing a tidy, stylish room. He dropped her on the bed then leaned over her, his hands pressed into the mattress on either side of her shoulders. "Dressed the way you are, I'd say you'd be more comfortable in a bed. Wouldn't you?"

"I thought we'd—"

Bending his elbows, he lowered his chest and face closer and whispered, "I want you here. In my bed. Now. We can play later."

Her breath caught in her throat. "Okay. Later."

He kissed her ear, pulling her earlobe into his mouth. His teeth nipped at the sensitive flesh. "I didn't think you'd complain."

A blanket of goose bumps covered her upper body and she shivered. "What's there to complain about, as long as you make yourself comfortable as well?" Her pussy throbbing, wet and achy, she lifted her feet and wrapped her legs around his waist. Her hands explored the rigid planes of his chest and stomach through his shirt before sliding down to pull the soft cotton knit up over his head. She gasped at the sight of his upper body uncovered. Thick arms with bulging biceps and triceps. Defined shoulders, a broad chest with chiseled pecs and a stomach most men would only dream of having. Absolutely awe inspiring. "My God! How many hours a day do you spend in the gym?"

"Probably too many." He ground his pelvis into hers and teased her nipples through the lace of her bra with his fingertips. "I'm glad you like what you see."

Her back arched as she strained to push her breasts up into his hands. "Oh, I like what I feel, too."

"This?" He pinched then released.

"And this." She reached down and slipped her hand between their bodies to caress his erection through his clothes. "Don't you want to take those pants off yet?"

"In a bit. I'm more content to tease you first."

"Well, that's no fair!" She started to lever herself up, but he pushed her flat on her back then held her there by the shoulders.

"Let's play a game."

She struggled a little to test how firmly he intended on holding her. He didn't let her budge. "I thought you said we would play later."

He grinned and shrugged his shoulders. "I changed my mind."

She returned his grin with one of her own then reached up. "Changing one's mind is a woman's prerogative, not a man's."

"I never said I played by the rules." He leaned lower and nibbled on her neck, producing more goose bumps.

"And you expect me to play a game with you? A confessed cheater?" Hot and breathless, and anxious for more, she tipped her head to give him better access to her neck.

His kisses and licks and love bites traveled lower, to the cleft between her neck and collarbone then lower still to the valley between her breasts. He hooked the lace demi-cup with a fingertip and pulled, uncovering the full globe of her breast and her erect nipple. He blew a cool stream of air on it and she sighed. "Why not? I think you'll find out that losing a game with me is as much fun—if not more—than winning. So, what do you say?" One hand pressed firmly against her lace-covered pussy.

A moan rose up her throat. "How do you expect me to say anything when you're torturing me like this?"

"It isn't difficult to say 'yes'." One fingertip slipped into her panties and teased her lips.

"Yes," she gasped. "Oh. Yes. What game do you want to play?"

The same finger that had rimmed her pussy touched her mouth and she licked it, tasting her own musky-sweet flavor.

"I like to call this game 'Master, May I?'." He pulled her nipple into his mouth and bit gently then twirled his tongue round and round, licking away the sting. "Ready?"

For anything! "I…oh…I…"

"Sounds like a yes to me. You ask the question, and I'll tell you the answer."

"Question? What question?"

He chuckled and she opened her eyes to see his expression. His wicked-hot smile did nothing to help her regain her mental facilities. "Master, May I?"

"Master, May I what?"

"You have to supply the what."

"Oh!" A glimmer of comprehension lit up her brain. "Okay. Master, may I fuck you?"

He cupped her breast in his hand and caressed. "Oh, no. You're not nearly ready for that yet."

"Speak for yourself, buddy."

One hand still working over her breast, he slid the other one down her stomach and slipped it into the waist of her panties. His fingers stroked her clit, and she involuntarily pressed her pelvis up and spread her legs wider. "See? Not even close." He pulled his hand out of her panties and held it up as illustration.

"What are you talking about? I'm soaking wet down there."

"You're still able to speak."

"Ha! Barely."

"Try another one." He pulled the lace away from her other breast and nuzzled it, cupping it in his palm.

"Another what?"

"Another question."

"Oh, okay. Master, may I…oh…" She pushed her chest up as he pulled her nipple into his mouth and suckled. His hand returned to her pussy, his fingers stroking her outer lips through her panties until she was ready to beg him to remove them. "Master, may I take off my panties?" she finally whispered.

"No, you may not." His kisses ventured lower, over her stomach and down to the low-riding waistband of her lace underwear. He pushed her knees further apart and rubbed her pussy.

Chapter Seven

He didn't say what I think he did, did he? The air seeped from Britt's lungs, and dizzy and blind with the need to be filled, she tangled her fingers in his hair. She pulled. "What do you mean, no?"

"I mean I will take them off for you."

"Oh." She eased the tension on his hair but didn't release him completely. It was so soft, the curls so silky between her fingers they tickled her palms. She shifted her hips as she felt him pulling her panties down over her mound. And she gasped and moaned as he kissed the flesh exposed as he slowly, torturously slid them lower still until her thighs were drawn together by the material, trapping her throbbing pussy between them.

Gently removing her hands from his hair, he pulled on her ankles until her legs straightened. Then he pushed them up until her feet were high in the air. "Now there's a sight. So sexy. So sweet."

Her legs trembled as his tongue glided up and down her slit. "Oh, God." The muscles running along the backs of her legs stretched tight as rubber bands, she fisted the bed coverlet.

He slipped the panties up her legs and pulled them over her shoes. Finally, he pushed her legs apart and pushed two fingers deep inside her pussy.

She screamed at the welcome invasion, grateful for his slow but rhythmic strokes to her inner walls. Her knees bent and lifted toward her shoulders, she welcomed each thrust of his fingers with a slight tip of her pelvis.

His tongue danced over her clit, and waves of heat pulsed out from her center. And the flush of an impending climax warmed her face and chest.

Then, he stopped. "Oh, no you don't. You didn't ask."

She drew in a ragged breath and dropped her hand to her pussy. If he wouldn't finish the job, she'd do it for him.

He caught her wrist and pulled it aside, trapping it in a tight fist. "Although I'd love to watch you do that, I can't let you. Remember the game."

"Shit!" she cursed, so frustrated and lost in her need she could barely think. "I'm so close. And I know this one's going to be powerful."

"Ask."

She inhaled against the urge to growl. Why was he making things so difficult? Didn't men love to watch a woman? Didn't they get off seeing a woman lose control? "Master, may I come?"

"No, you may not."

She slapped the mattress with her one free hand. "You never say yes!"

"I would if you asked the right question."

"Right. Wrong. Who the hell knows what's what at this point? All I know is that you've been teasing me and I'm hot, horny and ready to come. Isn't that a guy's wet dream? What are you waiting for?"

"I'm waiting for the right time."

"When will that be? I don't see it being any more right than now."

"What makes you think that?"

"I'm dying here. That's what. My heart is thumping so hard in my ears that I can barely hear you. My pussy's so hot that if you touch it again, it might combust. My breasts are so achy that I fear they'll never be the same."

"And what about your mind? Your spirit?"

"What about them? My mind's gone, lost in a fog. And spirit?"

"You see? You're so lost in the sensations of lovemaking that you've lost the connection."

"What connection? I'm confused." She dropped her feet to the bed and drew her knees together.

"Nope. Don't you dare close up. Not now." He caught her ankles and pushed them back and apart.

"I'm not. It's just hard to think when I'm hanging open like this."

"Try. I want you to understand. To me, sex isn't just about body parts, smells and sounds and touches. It's about souls and spirits and minds."

"Well, I can appreciate that. I don't do empty, meaningless sex, either. But in the midst of a climax, I'm afraid my spirit is the last thing I'm thinking about. Everything kind of closes in on me at that moment. And sensations take over."

He nodded and reached down to stroke her pussy, for which she was mighty grateful. "I understand. That's why at this point I've been concentrating on giving and not receiving."

"When will you receive?"

"Not today. I want today to be for you."

"No! What if I want you inside?"

"There are other things that are more important right now." He pushed two fingers inside her pussy and turning his hand, stroked the sensitive upper wall.

She groaned with the need to be filled completely.

"Do you trust me?"

"No," she teased, half meaning it. "You've done nothing but torture me since our first date. How could I?"

"Is that honestly how you feel?" His fingers slipped out, leaving her pussy achingly empty.

"No. I don't. I'm teasing you."

"So, you do trust me then?"

"Yes. Outside of teasing me to death, you've done nothing to make me distrust you."

"Good. I want to do something." He slid off the bed and walked to the closet. "Don't move."

Curious, but feeling a little strange lying flat on her back, her legs spread wide as if she were about to give birth, she watched him pull some metal rods from the bottom of the closet.

He returned to her side. "These are spreaders. They fasten on your thighs and wrists and hold them apart. Would you like to try them?"

Heat rose to her face. The idea of being tied up left her breathless and nearly ready to climax. Then he produced a large dildo and she squirmed with anticipation.

"And I think you know what this is."

"Yes. But can I see you first? Will you undress for me?"

"Maybe, after I secure you. I wouldn't want you taking advantage." He winked then reached for her wrist, his chest and upper body lowering until it hovered a fraction of an inch above her erect nipples. He secured both wrists in the leather straps then trailed a line of kisses and light bites down her torso.

Her eyes closed as she waited anxiously for him to strap her thighs.

"Uh-uh. I want you to watch me. Open your eyes. You cannot do anything without asking. Remember the game?"

"Master, may I close my eyes?"

"Nope. Watch." He kissed her inner thigh and her pelvis rocked rhythmically to the pounding of her heart. With a smile, he buckled the leather strap and pulled the second leg into place. Before strapping that one, he lowered his head and tongued her clit with quick jutting movements until her breath came in short, shallow gasps.

"Oh, God!"

"Don't come. You didn't ask. And I said to keep those eyes open."

She swallowed a scream of frustration and forced her eyelids to lift, not even aware they'd closed. "I hate this game!"

At least she was rewarded for the effort it took to focus her vision. On his knees, Andre slid down the zipper on his pants and pushed them down before flipping onto his back to remove them completely. His snug athletic boxers housed a huge bulge that she couldn't wait to see.

He returned to a kneeling position and pulled down the tight black cotton, releasing a very impressive, very large erect cock. Her hands wriggled against their bindings, itching to caress it, to grip it, to glide up and down its length. She licked her dry lips.

He shook his head, gripped his cock in his hand and gave it several smooth pumps. "This isn't for you yet." Then he picked up the dildo. "But this will be almost as good. Are you ready?"

"Hell, yes! Though I wish I was getting the real thing. My God!"

"Patience, love."

"I told you. I'm impatient."

He grinned. "I know." Then without warning, he parted her labia and pushed the dildo deep into her pussy.

Her fingernails dug into her palms as her entire body stiffened. "Oh!"

"Look at me." His expression intense, he pulled the dildo out then plunged it inside again. "Do you see how much I want you? Your pussy is so tight. So hot and wet. I'm going to come just watching you."

"Oh, God!" Her thigh muscles bunched into tight spasms and pulses of heat radiated up and out from her pussy. The sound of her juices as the dildo slid in and out echoed in her ears. The smell of her own arousal filled her nostrils. The sight of his hungry gaze on her pussy burned into her memory. "Master, may I…?"

"What, love?"

Her blood pulsed through her body in hot bursts, up through her chest, to her face. Her breathing ceased. "Come?"

"Yes, love. Come for me," he said, sounding as breathless as she felt. "Come for me now." He pushed a finger into her ass just as the first spasm of her climax blazed through her pussy. He groaned.

Heart-stopping spasms racked her body as it clenched and unclenched in time with her pussy. She felt her heart take flight, her soul and spirit. They rocketed through space and time, whirling, dancing, twining around a vivid blue light until the light opened and let her in.

And then, awash in a warm glow, she descended, back into her body. Onto Andre's bed, by his side. Little twitches skittered through her and a goofy sense of giddiness made her giggle.

A shiver reminded her she was cold but she didn't want to move yet. It was as if she was still in the middle of a wonderful dream, and she feared if she opened her eyes it would end.

"How do you feel?"

"Wonderful." She listened to the rattle of metal as he unfastened her wrists and thighs. Soft kisses took the place of the leather straps.

"Thank you," he said. "Thank you for giving so much of yourself. For trusting me." Dropping to his side, he pulled her to him until her entire body was crushed up against his. She sighed at the warmth and at the wonder of how great it felt in his embrace. Something slick and wet made her skin cling to his.

Never had a climax touched her the way that one had. And he still hadn't actually been inside her yet.

"Oh, and sorry about the mess," he murmured as he stroked her hair.

"What mess?"

"On your stomach. It's pretty wet. Let me get a washcloth."

"No!" She wrapped her arms around his chest and clung to him. "Just stay here a minute more. Please?"

"Okay." He chuckled. "If you insist. I thought you might be uncomfortable."

"Nope. I'm great. Just being with you like this. It's wonderful."

"Does that mean you'll stay the night? It's almost eleven. If you're going home, we need to get moving."

"If you're inviting me to stay, I'm game." She nuzzled his chest, enjoying the distinct scent of sex and man she found there. "Just make sure to set the alarm for early. I'll want a nice long shower in the morning before I head out to work."

"No problem. I have to be out early, too. We can conserve water." He winked.

A fresh wave of tingles washed over her body. Closing her eyes, she fell asleep, dreaming about sharing a shower with a sexy man with a hot body and the most beautiful eyes she'd ever seen.

*****

Unfortunately, thanks to the fact that Britt couldn't sleep soundly, she woke late. That meant there was no time for the leisurely shower with Andre she'd hoped for. Instead, she dashed home to change and arrived at work with no more than a second to spare.

Work was boring, as usual. The office was empty. All the salesmen were out making calls on clients. The phones didn't ring. But her memories of the previous night, Spider Solitaire, and a half dozen caffeine-loaded diet sodas were enough to keep her awake. By lunchtime, she was jittery, thanks to all the caffeine she'd consumed. But she wasn't in the best of moods, especially when she met up with Mary at the restaurant, and Mary had *the look* on her face the minute she sat down.

What disaster would it be this time?

"Are you going to tell me, or are you going to torture me?" Britt asked when Mary didn't say a word after at least five minutes. Mary was never quiet for that long. Not even in a movie theater.

Mary peered over the menu and blinked. "I'm not sure how to tell you this."

"Quit hiding." Britt pulled the menu away from Mary's face. "You look like a lost kitten. What are you scared of?"

"Nothing. Well, that's not true either. I'm worried. I've never seen you go so crazy over a guy before. You spent the night with him last night, didn't you?"

"Maybe." Britt tried to look nonchalant as she stirred her iced tea, but she knew she was failing. Mary knew her better than she knew herself. And even Britt knew she never spent a work night with a man.

"You're serious about him, aren't you?" Mary pulled the menu back over her face, leaving only her eyes and forehead exposed again.

"Would you quit doing that? And no, I'm not serious about him, yet. It's too soon."

"I don't believe you. And I'm afraid you'll go a little berserk when you hear this."

"Oh, for God's sake, just spit it out. I'm not married to the man. If it's something important, I need to know."

"Okay." Mary lowered the menu and leaned forward. "There's another woman," she whispered.

"Really?" Britt wasn't convinced. Surely Andre—Mr. Let's-be-honest and I'm-looking-to-settle-down—wouldn't have kept something that important from her. Heck, when did he have the time to see the other woman? "What makes you say that?"

"I talked to her at the club."

The club? A little twinge of suspicion slid up Britt's spine. "Maybe she's lying."

"Maybe. Then again, maybe she isn't. I had to tell you. I figured you have the right to know some woman—and let me tell you, she's gorgeous, not that you aren't—is running around saying she's involved with Andre."

For the most part, Britt didn't believe what Mary said, but a very small part of her had some doubts. She recalled that first night at the BDSM club, the buxom blonde in latex who'd tapped Andre on the shoulder. He'd known that woman, hadn't tried to hide it. *What if all that talk about settling down and commitment…and my soul…and trust…was just talk? I haven't known him for long. Am I being a fool for trusting him?*

"I appreciate your telling me. But we're not engaged or anything. I don't have any right to stake a claim on him. I have no right to be jealous."

"You don't expect me to believe you're okay with this."

Britt shrugged again. "What am I supposed to do? We've only seen each other a couple of times. I can't demand to know his every move."

"Find out the truth, so you know."

"Fine. I'll ask him if he's dating anyone else. Will that make you feel better?"

"You know, I told you only because I care. I like Andre…er, at least what I've seen so far. I want you to be happy."

"I know."

"When are you going to see him next?"

"Friday." Britt slid lower into her seat and guzzled her iced tea, knowing she wouldn't get a decent night's sleep until then. Friday couldn't come soon enough. And until then she couldn't get enough caffeine if it was pumped into her veins through an IV.

Chapter Eight

By the time Andre's car had pulled in Britt's driveway Friday night, Britt was again a miserable bundle of nerves. There was definitely a pattern developing.

Although now she wasn't afraid Andre would lock her in a cage or mercilessly torture her. This time, her fears surrounded a more delicate matter—one that involved her heart. She knew, in her current state, it was far easier for her heart to be crushed than for her body to be.

Regardless of what she thought she wanted, it was too late. She had developed feelings for Andre. Strong feelings she could no longer deny. Not only was he a giving lover, warm and tender and sexy, but also seemed to be a genuinely nice guy. He talked to her. He listened. He wanted to know how she felt, what she thought. It was impossible to have a casual relationship with him. He encouraged more, pulling her in slowly.

She could see what he was doing, dropping bits of bait to lure her closer, to gain her trust, but she couldn't stop herself. The bait was so…compelling.

He smiled as she opened the front door, his gaze wandering up and down her form. "You look incredible. I have a surprise for you." His expression eager, full of childlike excitement, he reached for her hand.

Curious, she pulled the door closed behind her, stepped onto the porch, and took his hand. "What kind of surprise?"

Taking long, quick strides, he pulled her toward the car. "If I told you, it wouldn't be a surprise. You'll just have to wait."

"Are you testing my patience again?" She sat in the passenger seat and looked up at him, catching his gaze as it dropped to her chest. Without looking down, she knew what he was staring at. The V-neck top she wore provided a nice view of her cleavage. A warm blush settled over her face.

He licked his lips. "Maybe. But you won't have to wait long." Before she could respond, he shut her door, walked around the front of the car, slipped into the driver's seat and closed the door. The car's engine roared to life as he turned the key.

Shifting into reverse, he glanced over his shoulder. "You're a little quiet tonight. Is everything okay?"

This was it, her opportunity to bring up the topic of dating other people. If she could just put aside that one worry, she could genuinely enjoy the process of getting to know Andre better. She could let herself fall in love with him. "To tell you the truth, I'm a little nervous."

"Again?" He shifted the car into first and hit the gas. "What's wrong?"

She pulled a deep breath into her lungs, knowing it was likely to be the last deep breath she'd take in a while. Past experience suggested when she was involved in a tense discussion, she tended to hyperventilate. "I…uh…" She glanced down at her hands, noting a slight tremble. She tried to remind herself that she couldn't avoid asking the question that was weighing so heavily on her heart. It was impossible. She'd go downright insane if she didn't. Things were moving too quickly not to know which direction they were headed. "I just need to get something straight."

He glanced at her then returned his gaze to the road. "Okay. What do you need to know?"

"You said you're looking to eventually settle down, but—" She stopped herself. *This is stupid! We've only gone on two, er, three dates. What man would make a commitment after such a short time? Why would I want that, either? I hardly know the man. He's a free agent, and so am I. We can date anyone we well want to, including beautiful blondes with perfect bodies…that I'd love to hate.* "Oh, forget it. Let's just go have some fun. That's what we're supposed to be doing. Right? Just have fun and get to know each other. No strings. No pressure."

He stopped the car at a red traffic light and studied her with narrowed eyes. "No strings? Am I going too fast for you?" The light turned green, and he pulled away, smoothly shifting gears. First, second, third.

"No. You're not going too fast."

"Are you sure?"

"Yes."

"Then why did you bring up the no-strings thing? That's not something I expected to hear from you."

"Why's that?"

"Because we've been pretty intense—at least I thought we have been. If you're looking for something casual…hmmm…" He let his sentence trail off unfinished and silently drove for a mile or two, and she remained silent, too.

What should she say? How could she explain what was going on inside of her? His words suggested he wasn't looking for a casual relationship. That was encouraging. Had her doubts been unfounded? Was she just buying a lie fed to her indirectly through a friend? Was the woman from the club just trying to scare her off? Andre's actions spoke volumes. He never spoke of other women. He never looked at other women when they were out. He never talked about being free or wanting space.

Quite the opposite. He seemed to be focused on one woman. Her.

The heaviness in her heart lifted slightly.

Moments later, he drove the car into a parking lot in front of a small dance studio. As he exited the car and opened her door, his expression remained friendly but lacked its former obvious glee. "I hope you enjoy my surprise."

"Are we taking dance lessons?"

"A close friend of mine owns this place. She offered to teach us a few moves. I thought you might enjoy it." He took her hand and together they walked across the empty parking lot.

"That's very romantic," she said, impressed by his sentiment. But as he pulled the door open for her, the rest of the compliment she'd meant to say lodged in the middle of her throat.

There, behind the front desk, stood the blonde from the club, decked out in a black leotard with a low scooping neckline that emphasized the size of her ample chest.

Taken off guard, Britt stepped backward but was stopped by Andre's bulk behind her.

"Britt," Andre said, "this is Stacy. Stacy and I have been friends since college. Stacy, this is Britt."

A genuinely warm smile on her face, Stacy stepped from behind the counter and offered Britt her hand. "It's very nice to meet you finally. Andre has told me so many great things about you."

"He has?" Studying Stacy's face for some sign of deception, Britt hesitantly took Stacy's hand and gave it a quick shake. But as she tried to pull her hand free, Stacy's grip didn't release. And then she realized something very shocking.

Stacy was checking her out! And she seemed to appreciate what she saw.

Britt didn't know how she felt about that. Relief—knowing Stacy wouldn't be interested in Andre if she was gay—and discomfort. Maybe even a little bit aroused.

"Are you ready to begin your lesson?" Stacy released Britt's hand and motioned toward a room to the right. "Follow me." She walked in front of Britt, flipping her long hair over her shoulder and swaying hips sparsely covered by leotard, opaque tights, and translucent skirt. Only a few steps behind, Britt had to admit that the woman did have a to-die-for body—not that she was attracted or anything.

In the center of the room, Stacy spun around unexpectedly, and Britt nearly walked straight into her. "Andre suggested ballroom lessons. Would you like that or something else? He said it's entirely up to you."

Feeling very clumsy, Britt halted suddenly then staggered, trying to catch her balance. "What other kinds of lessons do you offer?"

"All the usual. Tap, jazz, ballet. We also offer ballroom, belly dancing—"

"Belly dancing? I've always wanted to learn to belly dance."

Stacy gave her an appreciative smile. "Belly dancing it is, then. Andre? Do you want to watch?"

"Hell, no," he answered from behind Britt.

Assuming he was leaving, Britt turned toward him to thank him for the thoughtful gift. But, as she faced him, she realized by the way he was swinging his hips he had no intention of leaving.

And then his words reaffirmed that assumption. "I'm staying. I want to learn, too. Sounds like fun."

Stacy laughed. "Why does that not surprise me?" She walked across the room to a small closet and opened the door, pulling out some fabric. She shook out one piece then handed it to Britt then found a second one—a lovely shade of bubblegum pink—for Andre. "Tie these low around your hips, like a sarong skirt."

Britt secured hers over her jeans then watched Andre struggle to tie his over his khaki pants. Unable to stop herself, she giggled. "Do you need some help?"

Andre lifted his hands in defeat, and in a mockingly feminine voice he said, "They say these things are one-size-fits-all, but they never are."

That was it. Britt burst out in laughter, and Stacy joined her. Between the two of them, they managed, between fits of body-quaking hilarity, to tie the skirt around Andre's hips.

Then Stacy turned on the stereo and the room filled with the sound of Turkish music.

Not surprising to Britt, the lesson went very quickly. Stacy occasionally stepped up to Britt and laid her hands on her hips or stomach to help her learn a movement. But the touches, which normally would bother her because they were from a strange woman, had a very different effect. By the end of the lesson, thanks to Stacy's gentle strokes and Andre's flirty escapades, including a few maneuvers that reminded her of lovemaking, Britt was warm and tingly all over.

And the heaviness in her heart had nearly completely lifted.

Even while in a room with a woman who looked like she belonged on the cover of a swimsuit magazine, Andre's eyes were on Britt only. His playful smile was directed toward her only. His flirty innuendos were whispered in her ear only.

More than that, Britt could see the depth of his feelings in his eyes as he watched her dance. There was no hiding it. He didn't even seem to try. He was falling in love with her.

When Stacy announced the lesson was officially over, a flush-faced Andre thanked Stacy for the lesson, then turned toward Britt and drew her into a hug. One hand dropped to her bottom. "Did you have fun?"

Fighting a shudder as he squeezed her ass, she forced out, "Yes, I really did. I've always wanted to learn belly dancing."

"You're a natural. And you're always welcome to come back for more lessons—on the house," Stacy offered.

"Really? Wow, thanks!" Moving carefully, hoping to avoid making Andre release her, Britt pulled the knot at her hip loose and handed the scarf-like material back to Stacy. "But I feel like I should pay something." Andre began trailing tiny kisses down her neck. Carrying a conversation with Stacy while Andre produced goose bumps on top of goose bumps was no simple task. "I…uh…"

"No way." Stacy shook her head, her expression stern. "I would never charge a…friend…of Andre's. You'll just have to come after hours. Here's my card. Call me and we'll set up a time."

"Okay." Without reading it, Britt slid the card into her back pocket.

Andre gave Britt's shoulder a final bite then said, "Better get going. Dinner's ready at home. Hope you don't mind a home-cooked meal." He removed his skirt then took Britt's hand. "Do you mind if Stacy comes over, too? I kind of offered it as payment for the lesson."

"Oh, no! Not at all. That's the least we should pay. Heck, seeing you in a skirt was worth a hundred dinners." She chuckled at the memory of his comical attempts at a belly roll.

Andre kissed her nose, then whispered, "Just don't tell anyone. I'd never live it down." He gave her cheek a final caress with his thumb, then steered her toward the door by the shoulders.

"Who would I tell?" Britt called over her shoulder as she headed out the front door first, followed by Andre, then Stacy.

She rode in Andre's car while Stacy drove her own.

Warm all over, thanks to Andre, and energized from the exertion of dancing, she turned to him as he drove. "Stacy seems very nice."

"She's been a very good friend for a long time. But I want you to know, she's gay."

"I figured that out already."

"Does that bother you?"

"No, actually, I'm a little relieved," she admitted, watching his face for a reaction.

His eyebrows rose in a classic illustration of surprise. "Why's that?"

"I thought you were dating her."

He smiled and glanced at Britt. "A lot of people have made that assumption. She's a beautiful woman. And I admit we spend a lot of time together. But I'm not her type and she's not mine." He turned his head forward again. "I don't date more than one woman at a time, anyway. I'm a terrible juggler and an even worse liar."

"That's good to know."

"Yeah. When I try to lie, I break out in hives. My throat swells up." He closed his hand around his throat to illustrate. "It's not a pretty sight. I've learned to avoid lying at all costs."

"I can appreciate that. I'm a terrible liar, too."

"Um, there is one thing I want to tell you about Stacy, though."

Unsure whether she wanted to hear what was coming next, she reluctantly said, "Oh? What would that be?"

"Like I said, I'm a one-woman man, but Stacy would like to play with us a little."

One-woman man? A terrible juggler? Yet you're asking to invite another woman into the bedroom with us? Images of Andre and Stacy fucking in front of her passed through her mind, and she immediately hated the idea. "Oh. I don't know."

"I won't touch her and she won't touch me."

"I guess I'm not sure what she'd do then. Oh!" A few pieces of the puzzle dropped into place, and her face heated. *She's gay.* "Wait a minute. You mean she'd do stuff to me?" A warm wave rocketed through her body.

"Only what you're willing to let her do. She's a slave. She does as she's told."

Confused, but also intrigued, Britt turned and stared blindly out the window. *Oh my God! Another woman? Me?* "I've never… I don't know." She tried to imagine what it would be like to have Stacy touching her breasts, her pussy.

Her body's instant reaction was impossible to ignore. Her heartbeat raced, her body tingled, her pussy throbbed. Uncomfortable, thanks to the heat radiating from between her legs, she shifted in her seat and opened the car window a crack. *I'm not a lesbian. Why does the idea of this turn me on so much?*

"It's your decision. I won't force you to do anything you don't want to."

"Okay. I'll think about it," she agreed, knowing already what the answer would be.

There was something about having another woman touching her, watching as Andre made love to her. Her panties were becoming more soaked by the second.

Much to her surprise, Britt wanted to try it.

*****

Dinner—a luscious slow-cooked roast and potatoes—was accompanied with friendly, animated chatter. Andre seduced Britt with heated glances and flirty winks. His hand rested possessively on her knee throughout most of the meal, occasionally wandering higher to caress between her legs. The teasing touches drove her crazy with desire.

Stacy gave her one or two heated glances, seeming to try not to be too forceful or intimidating.

After they'd laughed, and eaten, and exhausted all casual conversation, Andre cleared the dishes and announced, "How about we go downstairs for a while?"

Stacy, who sat to Britt's left, turned to glance at her, an unspoken question on her face. Britt knew this was it, her final opportunity to back out. A momentary panic gripped her right around the throat, leaving her speechless.

Stacy looked at Andre. "I should probably go. Maybe another time?"

"No," Britt forced the word past the mountain blocking her trachea. "I want you to stay."

Stacy answered her request with a beaming smile. She stood and reached for Britt's hand. "It'll be okay. Better than okay. I promise."

"I promise, too. Trust me," Andre said, motioning her toward the kitchen.

Andre's hand clasped around her right hand, Stacy's around her left, she descended the stairs at the rear of the kitchen slowly, unsure of what to expect.

The minute they reached the playroom, Stacy excused herself to change her clothes, leaving Andre and Britt alone.

Andre pulled Britt into an embrace, resting one palm on her cheek while pressing the side of her face against his chest. She let his heart's slow, steady beat soothe her quickly frazzling nerves. "I know this is your first time. I want it to be memorable, not scary."

She nodded.

He palmed both her cheeks and turned her face to his. Two brown eyes with flecks of gold stared straight into hers. "Listen to me closely. If either of us do anything you don't like, I want you to tell me. Okay? Pick a safe word. Something you will remember. Something you wouldn't normally say during lovemaking."

"Tomato?"

He chuckled and nodded. "When I hear the word tomato, I'll stop whatever I am doing, and so will Stacy. I want this to be a very intense experience for you, but also pleasant, special."

"I have a feeling it will be."

Stacy returned to the room wearing the same black latex catsuit she'd worn at the club. The center zipper was unfastened down to her navel, exposing a V of tanned skin and the inner curves of her breasts. "Is everything okay?" Her gaze hopped back and forth between Britt and Andre.

Andre nodded. "The word is tomato."

"Got it." Stacy stepped closer, approaching Britt almost as if she were approaching a scared child. But instead of touching Britt, Stacy dropped to her knees before Andre, bent her head forward, and remained still, one hand resting on each thigh. "Master."

Here I go! No turning back, now.

Chapter Nine

Not sure what she should do, but having an inkling, she glanced at Andre for a cue.

He smiled then nodded slowly, and she dropped to her knees beside Stacy and repeated, "Master." It felt a little unnatural, like she was putting on a show, but she took the role of slave and waited for Andre's next move.

He rested his hands on the top of her head. "It pleases me to see you submitting at last, Britt. However, when you come to me, I expect you to be completely unclothed. You may hide nothing from me."

"Oh. Sorry. I didn't know. We didn't go over the rules yet." She started to pull her top over her head.

"No. Stop."

Britt released her shirt, the bottom hem around her shoulders.

"Stacy will undress you."

"Oh." Her heart beating in her ears, she dropped her arms and turned toward Stacy. She closed her eyes.

"No, Britt. Open your eyes. Look at Stacy."

She stared at Stacy's face, surprised to see an almost complete lack of emotion. The woman looked more like a nurse than a lover. Her unaffected expression slowed Britt's racing heart a bit. *It's just like being at the doctor's office.*

Stacy pulled Britt's top over her head, then reached around to unhook her bra, pulling each shoulder strap down until the garment fell on the floor. Then she unzipped Britt's jeans and pulled them over her hips.

"Lie down, Britt," Andre commanded.

She lay on her back and lifted her hips to allow Stacy to pull her shoes and jeans off. Then Stacy hooked her fingers under Britt's underwear and pulled.

Britt glanced at Andre, not sure if he expected her to remain lying down or return to kneeling. Meanwhile, Stacy resumed her obedient pose, head down, hands resting on thighs.

"Much better, Britt. Now, to assure you won't forget, you will pay the consequences for coming before me fully clothed."

Uh, boy! Here it comes. Her pussy tingled as Andre's hot gaze raked over her flesh. She felt her skin warming.

"Stand up," he demanded.

Both Britt and Stacy stood.

"Stacy, place Britt on the spanking bench."

"Yes, Master." Stacy took Britt's hand and led her to a piece of furniture that slightly resembled a weight bench. With hands on Britt's shoulders, she coaxed her to kneel on the floor then rest her upper body on the leather seat part. Then she pulled Britt's knees apart and secured Britt's wrists in leather cuffs.

By the time Britt was in position, her pussy was throbbing with expectation. Stacy pushed lightly on Britt's back, encouraging her to arch it and tip her ass up in the air.

She'd never felt so exposed, so out of control. It was a wonderful, erotic feeling. Her entire body was energized, her blood pumping hot as acid through her body. Her breaths failed to fill her hungry lungs.

And then she felt the slap, and in a heartbeat a sharp stinging pain warmed her backside. She squirmed, breathless, and tried to look over her shoulder to prepare for the next one.

"No. Look forward."

She obediently stared straight ahead.

"Arch that back."

She arched her back, lifting her smarting ass as high as she could.

"And relax the muscles."

She forced herself to slacken her ass muscles.

A second swat sounded in her ears, and another rush of biting pain razored up her spine. She gasped at both the pain and the pleasure ripping through her body, gripped the chains holding her wrists to the underside of the bench, and forced herself to hold her position.

"Very nice, Britt. What have you learned?"

"To come before you undressed."

"Very good."

A soft touch smoothed over her bottom, cooling the heat. "You have a perfect ass. So full and round." Fingers dipped between her ass cheeks, teasing her anus, and she reflexively tipped her hips higher giving him better access. "Oh, yes. Just like that. Your hole is so tight. I want to fuck it."

Recalling the size of his cock, she shuddered. "I've never…you're so big."

"Trust me. I won't hurt you."

She dropped her head to the bench, tipping it to the side and relishing the cool touch to her flaming face. "Yes, Master."

"Good! I want to reward your trust. Stacy, the beads."

"Yes, Master," Stacy responded.

The hands that had been soothing Britt's ass lifted and Britt wondered whose they had been.

A moment later, Britt felt a touch to her ass again, fingers pulling her cheeks apart.

"Your ass is perfect. So tight and smooth. Have you ever had anal beads before, Britt?"

"No," she whispered, completely aroused at the soft exploring touches. Fingers probed her pussy, slipping up to circle over her clit before dipping down into her vagina. More touches wandered up and down her crack.

"Your pussy is so smooth since you shave."

Hands messaged her thighs with strong pressure, working out knots she hadn't known were there. More hands worked over her ass and pussy, stroking, teasing, fingers dipping inside.

She moaned at the sensation overload. The feel of hands all over her pussy and ass and legs. The sound of her own shallow breaths in her ears. The scent of oils. "Yes."

"For that you'll be rewarded as well."

"Thank you."

Fingers pulled her ass cheeks apart, exposing her anus, and then something pushed at the barrier.

"Open to me, Britt."

She tried to force her muscles to relax against the pressure, to allow whatever was pushing inside. It was nearly impossible. Her entire body was tensing as waves of heat pulsed up and out. The pace of each wave increased with each heartbeat.

And then she felt a pop as the first bead slid inside, filling her anus. She gasped, her pussy throbbing, juices dripping down the front and cooling her skin. "Oh!"

"I want to reward you some more," Andre said.

"Yes! More."

Another bead slipped inside, giving a slightly increased feeling of fullness. It was a very pleasant, erotic feeling. "More?"

"Yes!"

A third bead popped inside and her fingernails dug into her palms as she fought to control the rush of tingling heat radiating through her body. Climax was just on the horizon. She could feel it.

"Release her hands."

Stacy kneeled beside her, releasing first one hand, then the other.

"Turn over, Britt. With your ass on the opposite end. You have been very, very good. You deserve another reward."

Dizzy from the rewards she'd already received, and not sure how many more rewards she could take, she turned around and lay on her back. Stacy lifted her ankles and strapped them high in cuffs suspended from the ceiling.

Legs spread in a wide V, Britt watched and waited as Andre pulled down his pants and unwrapped a rubber. He pulled it over his erection, then kneeled. The bench was the perfect height.

She arched her back, silently pleading for him to fill her.

Stacy kneeled to one side.

"Another bead." He pulled his cock away slightly and Stacy lifted her hands to Britt's anus, pushing a final bead inside.

Breathless with the urgent need to be filled, out of her mind with arousal, she watched Stacy touch her. Stacy's hand wandered higher, her fingers dipping into Britt's pussy before circling over her clit.

It was too erotic to watch. Britt dropped her head back and closed her eyes, intent to concentrate on the touches to her pussy and the fullness in her ass.

"Is she ready for me yet?" Andre asked.

"No, Master."

"Slacken the chain. I want her knees bent, her legs wider."

"Yes, Master," Stacy answered.

The tension on Britt's legs eased, allowing her to lower her ankles. A gentle push on her knees forced them apart and high up on either side of her body.

Oh, so wide. So hot. Fuck me!

Britt felt she would go insane if he didn't give her release. Her entire body was pulling into tight knots. She couldn't breathe or think. Sensations were blurring into colors and sounds. She tasted the musk of her own arousal as it filled the air.

Then, fingers pulled her labia apart and a warm tongue flickered over her clit, sending white-hot bolts of desire up to her belly.

Andre's cock pushed inside, stopping just inside before filling her completely and stretching her vagina.

She thrashed her head back and forth, her eyelids clamped tight. Her stomach muscles spasmed and her feet curled. "More!"

His cock pushed another fraction of an inch inside and she consciously tightened her vaginal walls around it, savoring the increased sensation. She was so close, so very close! Cold and hot zipped up and down her body as the throb of her impending climax took hold of her.

"Now," Andre shouted.

And as the first spasm of orgasm gripped Britt's body, he thrust his cock deep inside. That, with the added sensation as the first bead slid out of her ass, magnified her climax until she lost all control. Andre's cock thrust in and out, in and out as her pussy spasmed around it. And with each thrust, a bead was pulled out of her ass.

She screamed with release, so overcome by the sensations pummeling her body to sort one out from the other. Then she felt the swelling of Andre's climax, and he growled before thrusting inside her one final time.

And then breathless, dizzy and disoriented, she opened her eyes.

Stacy smiled at her and unable to speak, she smiled back.

Andre pulled out, removed the condom and unbuckled the straps holding Britt's legs, then pulled her to him in a tight embrace. "How do you feel, Britt?"

She took stock of the various sensations and emotions still rushing through her body. "Overwhelmed." She watched as Stacy stood and silently left the room.

Andre stood and led her upstairs. "In a good way?"

"Oh, yes. Where's Stacy going?"

He led her into his bedroom and lying down, pulled her into the bed with him. "Home. She only came here to serve you. Her task is done now."

She rested her head on his chest and curled up against his warmth. "I've never had an experience like that before, with another woman."

"Did you like it?"

"Honestly, I wasn't sure what she was doing and what you were doing. But the whole thing was incredible."

"Good. I'm glad you enjoyed it."

"Very much."

"I'm not your average Master. You see, we're bending the rules to meet our needs. Do you like our game? Would you like to play again with me?"

"Oh, yes! Couldn't you tell?"

"Then I have to ask you for a promise." His fingertip pulled at her chin until she tipped her face toward his.

"What promise?"

"I know it hasn't been long, but I want you."

Not sure if she understood him correctly, she asked, "What are you saying?"

"I want to make a commitment to you. Right here. Right now. Britt, I'm falling in love with you. I may play your Master in the bedroom, but you own my heart. For always. I've wanted this since the first time I saw you."

Tears burned Britt's eyes as she read the truth in his.

"My heart is yours, Britt," he repeated. "Thank you for being so willing to open up to me, to share your thoughts and fears and joys with me. I hope you want to do that for a lifetime."

She swiped at a hot tear as it slid down her cheek. "Thank you for helping me learn how to open up. You've shown me how to be a better person. How to explore and share. How to love." She chuckled. "I had no idea that paddles and spreaders and swings could do that, teach such deep lessons. You were right. It's more than dominating another human's body. It's about learning about yourself and each other. Encouraging each other to grow and learn. My heart is yours, too, Andre. Forever."

That night, they stayed up all night, making love…and planning their future, together.

A Game of Risk

Chapter One

Today was a day to celebrate. It was one of those days that made up for the misery of the past several weeks—in all ways.

Olivia reclined in her chair and propped her feet on her desk between two stacks of printouts and a mountain of bills, content to stare at her computer screen for a few more minutes. No need to head to the recruiter's office in search of a boring day-job yet. No need to call her creditors and beg for extensions, either. Her latest stock pick had paid off—huge!—and paying her bills wouldn't be a problem for at least a couple of months.

Thank you, Lord!

She knew most everyone in her circle, friends and family both, thought she was nuts. Quitting a lucrative job working for one of the most powerful investment firms in the country and doing the unthinkable—gasp!—day trading at home looked like financial suicide to them. But Olivia knew she had what it took to make it. She knew the market, had proven it time and time again by making her clients filthy rich. She was due a little of that wealth now, and this was the only way she'd get it.

Yes, the market wasn't what it had been a few years ago. Bear or Bull, each had its opportunities. It was just a question of knowing how to take advantage of them.

Today was a prime example. She stared at the screen and sighed. It had been almost as good as sex…if she remembered what sex was like. The opportunity for sex hadn't presented itself in a long time. Too long.

Cobwebs were growing between her legs. And that was a crime. No woman in her early thirties should have to endure month after month of abstinence. It wasn't natural.

If only she had a sex-friend, a guy she could make an agreement with. No-strings sex. That was what she was in the mood for tonight. Meaningless fucking. Oh, yes. A hard, muscular male body heavy on top of her, hands delving into regions that had gone unexplored for far too long.

Her pussy wetted at the thought, closing around the achingly familiar emptiness as she recalled how it felt to be fucked into oblivion. A sigh leapt from her chest.

She knew nothing that exciting would happen anytime soon. Tonight was girls' night. Lots of gabbing, bad movies, and noshing on fat-laden snacks. So, until she found Mr. Sex-for-now, she'd have to settle for the thrill of a profitable trade.

She leaned forward and read over the details of her recent transaction. Damn, that was exciting! Turning a thousand dollars into almost ten thousand was close to orgasmic. She smiled intently and listened to her racing heart thump in her ears.

After a while, the little black numbers finally lost their impact, and her breathing returned to normal. She headed to her bedroom to change, digging through the unfolded heaps of clothing on her bed. After today's bit of good news, there was nothing her sister and friends could do to bring her down. Even sitting around watching hours of depressing chick flicks wouldn't do it.

After dressing in a pair of hip-hugger jeans and a comfy sweatshirt, she went to the kitchen to prepare the food. The girls weren't fussy. A bowl of nacho chips, salsa, some spinach dip from the grocery store's deli and pita bread…and chocolate in any form…and all was ready. Then she made an attempt at straightening the living and dining rooms, stashing stacks of newspapers and books in baskets and under furniture.

The hens would be there any minute. *Cluck, cluck, cluck.* All but one was single, so the inevitable subject matter would be men, as it always was.

But tonight she didn't care.

Her sister, Evelyn—Eve for short—showed up at exactly seven. She was always punctual. Yes, according to their parents, Eve was unlike her older sister Olivia in most ways that mattered, responsible and levelheaded to start.

Olivia didn't mind their parents' constant disapproval. She'd endured it all her life. Heck, if they suddenly decided to be supportive, she wouldn't know how to react. A man who'd worked at the same steel plant since the day he'd graduated from high school and a woman who'd stayed home to raise two girls and poured her heart and soul into baking homemade cookies and not-from-a-box meals couldn't understand where she was coming from.

"Hey, Sis," Olivia greeted Eve as she stepped into her apartment.

"Liv, I have a surprise for you!" Eve thrust a box at Olivia's chest then slammed the front door behind her.

Olivia glanced down at the box as she followed Eve to the couch. "What's this? My birthday isn't for months."

"It's tonight's entertainment." Eve sat daintily and crossed her legs.

"Oh, yeah? What is it? A party-in-a-box?" She pulled the outer plain wrapping away revealing a colorful box with the words Private Games printed across the front.

"You could call it that. It's one of those party games. It sounded like fun. Of course, since it's for single women…" She glanced down at the three-carat rock on her finger and smiled. "I won't be able to play along. Wish I could. It sounds like a riot."

"Yeah," Olivia said, not buying Eve's exaggerated effort at disappointment. "Sure you do."

The other ladies showed up within minutes of each other, and in no time, Olivia's living room was brimming with female bodies and voices. The stereo, which Olivia had set to play some '80s dance music at a legal volume, was completely drowned out by the chatter.

Really, girls' night had become much too big. It had started out cozy, with three— Eve, Olivia and Olivia's neighbor, Ann. Then Eve had begun inviting her neighbors, a couple ladies from church, and they invited their friends, and so on and so on… There had to be fifteen women in her apartment tonight.

When the decibel level reached that of a jet engine's roar, Eve stood up, waved her arms and said, "I have an announcement. I brought a party game for anyone who is interested. I thought it would be a nice change from our usual. Olivia will set it up on the dining room table."

A mad rush of curious women headed toward the dining room. Olivia, carrying the box, followed them. She spread out the game board, pieces, and directions and motioned to the four women who voiced their interest in playing the loudest. They each took a seat. Olivia scanned the directions and laughed.

She had never backed down from a challenge, but this game was ridiculous! Still, as she glanced at the TV and saw that the rest of the group was watching *Fried Green Tomatoes*…again… she was willing to toss the dice and see where she landed.

It was only a game.

"Okay. Since I'm the hostess, I'll go last." She glanced at the woman to her right, Eve's next-door neighbor, Laura, a mousy brunette with a deadbeat ex-husband and a houseful of kids to raise by herself. "Would you like to go first?"

"Oh, no thanks! I couldn't."

"Oh, come on!" the woman to Laura's right said. "Go for it."

Laura smiled tensely and nodded. "Okay." She shook the dice and rolled then moved her piece two spaces to an empty square. She relaxed back into her chair and looked toward the woman who'd just coaxed her into making the first move. "You're next."

The woman, another one of Eve's neighbors, shook the dice and rolled a three which also landed her on an open square. This game wasn't proving to be very amusing. It had to get better than this, quick.

Her train of thought took a detour… Two ladies had taken their turns and so far no one had rolled higher than three. This was beginning to look suspicious. Were the dice loaded?

The third woman, a young member of Eve's church, rolled a two, her piece resting next to Laura's.

Finally, the fourth, a woman Olivia only knew as *B*, rolled something higher than three. And it landed her on a challenge space.

B drew a card and read it aloud, "Hand the next Challenge card to the player on your left. Both players will complete the challenge."

Olivia smiled and shook her head. "Just my luck! I haven't even thrown the dice and I'm losing already."

"Depends on how you look at losing," B said as she handed the top card from the deck to Olivia.

Olivia scanned it then read it aloud, laughing. "Contact your secret crush and tell him how you feel." She returned the card to the bottom of the deck and shrugged her shoulders. "I don't have a secret crush. That's for schoolgirls." She visually searched out her sister in the crowded living room. "Eve, are you sure this game isn't for kids?"

"Of course it's not. In fact it's rated *For Adults Only*, you liar!" Eve shouted from her seat on the couch. She jumped up and strode across the room. "And you do too have a crush. On my husband's big brother, Ty. I've seen you drooling over him, and it just so happens he's newly single."

Do not! "You set this up, didn't you? The game. The cards. Well, you wasted your time. I'm not the least bit interested in him. You sneaky little—"

"How could I set up anything? I had no idea who would play and who wouldn't."

"You know, it would have been easier just to plan a dinner out and *accidentally* bump into him at the restaurant."

Eve slapped her hand to her thigh. "Darn! I didn't think of that. Seriously, he's single and available. And you've drawn that card. Fair's fair. You have to call him."

"Fine, I will. Later. It's too loud in here. I couldn't have a conversation if my life depended on it."

Eve grinned and moseyed over to the wall phone. "If you don't call him, I will."

"Don't you dare."

She picked up the receiver and dialed. "It's ringing..."

"I can make my own phone calls, thank you." Olivia made a lunge for the lever, hoping to end the call before he picked up.

Eve caught her wrist and deflected her hand just before it cut off the call. Then she frowned. "Answering machine." She hung up. "You got lucky tonight, but I won't let this go. You'll thank me someday. He's a hottie. You haven't seen him in a while."

"A hottie? Since when? You know what?" Olivia turned to face the four women sitting at the dining room table watching her make a fool of herself, not that she hadn't done so before. "I should get back to being hostess. I have some...er, punch to mix. And look! The dip is empty! So sorry. I'm done with this game. You ladies can continue without me," she announced, suddenly in the mood to head to the nearest bar and get drunk. "One Challenge card's enough for me. I fold."

The remaining players didn't seem to mind the loss. They all smiled and continued playing. After accomplishing the tasks she'd successfully used to duck out of the game, Olivia found an empty spot on the couch and tried to enjoy a movie she'd seen at least a couple dozen times. She played friendly hostess, refilling depleted chips and dip and empty glasses for the next two hours, occasionally drawn to the dining room by raucous laughter and cheers, until one-by-one the ladies excused themselves, thanked her for the wonderful time, and left.

Then, in the mood to go out and celebrate her recent financial boon, she changed into her sexiest black dress, grabbed

Ann and asked her if she'd like to join her for a drink at the bar, and headed for the car. This was one Friday night she wouldn't let go to waste.

They took Ann's car, since it was her turn to be designated driver. And rather than driving across town to go to their favorite nightclub, they agreed to stay closer to home, choosing what looked like a cozy club only a few miles down the road.

As they walked into the bar, Ann asked, "What's up with you tonight? You're in a strange mood."

"I made one hell of a killing today. Sold AGH short. It fell like lead today after releasing first quarter losses. God, I love it when I'm right. I'm in the mood to celebrate!"

"Oh, wow! That's great! I guess I'd be a little restless if I'd had a day like that, too. How much did you make?"

"Oh, a few thousand dollars," Olivia responded, pulling open the bar's front door.

"I wish I could make that kind of money in a single day! I tried buying stocks once. It took me all of six months to lose every penny I'd invested."

"That's not difficult to do if you don't know what you're doing." Olivia stopped dead in her tracks as they entered the dark, tight interior of the bar. "This place isn't exactly what I thought it would be."

"Yeah. Me neither."

She scanned the almost entirely male clientele. Most of them had longer hair than hers. And there was more leather in the place than in Olivia's favorite store in the mall. Still, no one seemed to pay them any attention, and Olivia decided it would be safe enough to sit at the bar and have one drink.

The bartender, a burly man with a thick, gray beard gave them an appraising once-over. "Are you ladies lost?"

"Not really," Olivia settled on a stool. "I'll take a glass of your best wine."

"Our best is probably not up to your standards, but if that's what you'll have, I'm glad to oblige." His gaze jumped to Ann. "And you, little lady?"

"I'll take a cola, please."

"Sure 'nough." The bartender poured a glass of white wine from a nondescript bottle for Olivia and filled a glass with cola for Ann. "That'll be five dollars."

"Can you run a tab?" Olivia asked, lifting the glass to her nose.

"Are you sure about that?"

She sipped. The liquid had a bit of a rough bite, but nothing too intolerable. "The wine's not that bad. Yes, please. I prefer a tab. Do you need a credit card?"

"Naw. I don't think you're going to run off without paying. You don't look the type. Then again, you don't look the type that would come in here anyways. What are you two doing here tonight? I haven't had this much class at my bar since 1972."

"Really?" Olivia took another sip of her wine and set the glass on the paper napkin. "That long, eh? Thanks for the compliment."

"Seriously. Every woman not looking for trouble 'round here knows better than to come into this dump. Just make sure if you hear voices rising you duck in that corner." He motioned toward the nearest corner of the room. "Things are bound to start flying."

Olivia took another chance to appraise the inhabitants of the room. "Oh, this is one of those places! A...biker bar? I've never seen a real bar fight."

Ann gripped Olivia's forearm. "Maybe we should go somewhere else, Liv."

The bartender nodded. "If you stick around here long enough, you'll see plenty. Trust me."

Olivia wriggled her arm free from Ann's grip. "Everything's calm. No need to drink and run. This place is interesting. It has character—"

"Fuck you! You cheating bastard!" one guy yelled at the pool table in the rear of the bar.

The bartender did a Houdini, disappearing through a door in the back wall.

"That's our cue. Time to go, Liv." Ann pulled some money out of her purse and dropped it on the bar.

"No, it's just a friendly dispute. See? Everything's fine." She pointed at the two men, standing chest to chest, staring each other down like two rams with their horns locked. She turned around, facing the bar again. "I'm not running out of here like a chicken. My wineglass is still three-quarters full. Besides, those men wouldn't hurt an innocent woman. We're just sitting here minding our own business."

"I wouldn't count on that." Ann pulled out her car keys and fisted them. "If this gets ugly we're out of here."

"That's fine. I'm all for safety." Olivia casually sipped her wine.

"Ha! You?" Ann let loose a round of forced guffaws. "For fun, you jump from bridges, float down rapids in flimsy blow-up rafts, and leap from planes that aren't sitting on the ground. You have no use for safety. In fact, I'd say you have a death wish."

"I do not. I respect safety, within reason. I just don't want to leave if we don't have to. I think that bartender thought we were a couple of prissy suburban princesses. He's wrong. I can handle this. Don't forget, I grew up in a rough neighborhood. I made friends with the hookers at the end of our street."

"How could I forget when you remind me constantly?" Ann shook her head and shifted nervously on her stool.

"I do not...okay, I do, but not constantly." Olivia gave her friend an exaggerated scowl until a loud scuffle brought her attention to the room behind them once again. But before she could turn completely around, something wooden splintered.

Then it was pure chaos.

Loud voices shouting, glass breaking, wood furniture smashing. Fists and bodies flying.

"Oh, shit!" Ann shouted, catching Olivia's hand and giving it a swift jerk. They dropped from their stools, and glancing over their shoulders, half-ran, half-crawled toward the exit. Olivia laughed the entire way. "I can't believe you think this is funny," Ann muttered as she reached the door and stood to open it. "You have one sick sense of humor."

"It just reminds me of a bad movie. Sorry." Just before Olivia leapt out the door, something hit her from behind. A flash of white light and a blur of color shot before her eyes.

Then silence.

*****

"This is the third time this week we've been called here. I wish the city would just shut the place down," Ty Wilcox said as he gathered his supplies from the ambulance. "Do the police have the scene secured yet?"

"I think so. One told me it's a real mess in there," his partner Matt said, pulling out a backboard and grabbing a bag full of first aid supplies. "Ready?"

"Yeah." Ty followed him to the door and into the building, noticing the two young women lying on the floor just inside. Both were unconscious. Both were beautiful, and neither looked like they belonged in the Rusty Nail.

The blonde, wearing a clingy black dress with a hem that had inched its way up to her waist, moaned and blinked her eyes.

Ty dropped to a squat next to her, quickly assessing her legs and arms. No breaks or stab wounds. He palpated her abdomen. Soft. "It's okay. My name's Ty. I'm here to help. Where do you hurt?"

She lifted a shaky arm to her head. "The back of my head. Did you say Ty? I have a brother-in-law named Ty. And he's a paramedic, too."

Immobilizing her neck, he slid a gloved hand around the back of her head and felt a telltale warmth. Blood. "Yes. Do you remember your name?"

"Yes. Olivia. Olivia Blake."

"Olivia?" That was a familiar name. He studied her face, not sure if he would recognize her. They'd only met once. Was she? It couldn't be… Then again, how many Olivia Blakes could there be in one city, especially Olivia Blakes with brothers-in-law named Ty who happened to be paramedics. The law of averages was on her side. "Are you allergic to anything, Olivia?"

She grimaced. "Pain."

She's making a joke? Now? He remembered the wedding, the smart comeback she'd coolly dealt his date when they'd first met. The stinger had left one hell of a first impression, and had led to Karen's instant migraine no doubt. Granted, Karen hadn't been on her best behavior that night either.

"Do you feel sleepy?"

"A little. Now that you've come to my rescue, and I'm in your strong and very capable hands, can I take a nap?"

Cute. Evidently the blow to the head didn't impact her sense of humor. That cinched it. This comedienne was Eve's sister for sure. "No. Stay awake for me. Okay? Do you remember what happened?"

"Yeah. There was a fight and we were trying to leave. Then I felt something…my head is really hurting."

"Let me get a neck brace on you and then I can take a look. Do you hurt anywhere else? Stomach? Chest? Back?"

"No. Just my head. And I feel like I might throw up." Her lips paled.

He secured her neck then rolled her to her side. "Ummm. You have quite a bump there. Better come to the hospital and get it checked out."

"No. I hate hospitals. I'm fine. See?" Wincing and ashen, she struggled to sit up, one hand on her head. Her eyes lobbed from side to side as she rested against the wall. "Oh..."

"You're not fine. You could have a concussion and internal injuries. There's no way for me to assess that. You need to be checked out."

"No, I've just had too much cheap wine."

He lit his penlight and checked her pupils. Equal and reactive. Then checked her pulse. That was normal, too. Blood pressure was fine. "I'd still like you to come with me. Besides, you can't drive."

"That's okay. My friend is doing the driving tonight."

"You mean the lady over there?" He motioned toward the brunette still lying unconscious on the floor. Matt was working her up. "I don't think she'll be driving anywhere anytime soon, either."

Olivia strained to turn toward her friend. "Oh, my gosh! Is Ann okay?"

"She has an ugly knot on the head. She's going to the hospital," Matt said as he secured her on the backboard. "I'm going for the gurney."

"You think you can walk?" Ty asked Olivia. "If not, we'll have to wait until another unit is available." He glanced around the room. Several other EMT teams had arrived, but they were all busy assessing other patients.

"I think I can walk. With some help, maybe."

"Okay. Sit tight. I'll be right back." Ty assisted his partner as he lifted the brunette onto the gurney then returned to Olivia. "Feeling any better yet?" He ran his fingers down her spine, checking for obvious injuries.

"Not really."

"Okay. We'll take this slow." Standing, he hooked his arms under hers and lifted.

She swayed, her legs wobbly, and flopped against him. Then, she retched, emptying the contents of her stomach down his side.

He grimaced at the putrid warmth spreading down his side. Another uniform wasted. At least this time it was by a family member.

He held in a groan and waited for her to gather some strength.

"I'm so sorry," she muttered. "How embarrassing."

"You can't help it. Let's just get you to the hospital." He half-carried her to the ambulance and with help from Matt got her up into it. Then he gave Matt the go ahead to leave. "I'll stay in the back with the ladies."

Matt looked at Ty's soiled clothes and nodded. "Good idea." Within minutes, they were on their way to the hospital. Although Olivia was silent, monitoring the two patients kept Ty busy until they arrived at St. Joe's emergency room. And only after they'd been turned over to the hospital staff, did he have time to think about the call.

"What were those two doing in that dump?" he asked Matt as he changed into some burrowed scrubs and bagged his soiled uniform. "They were as out of place as two mice in a cat house. The blonde is my sister-in-law. My brother's married to her sister."

"Wow. Glad they'll be okay."

"Me, too. Hopefully they'll learn to stay out of places like that. What were they thinking? Jesus, I wish people would just use some common sense. So many catastrophes could be avoided if they did."

"Oh, no, that rampage again." Matt shook his head.

"Well, how many people do we have to dig out of a mess that they put themselves into?" He bent down to tie his shoes, thankful for the fact that her vomit had at least spared those.

"Call me stupid, but I figure women should be able to go into a bar and not be clubbed over the head."

"They don't belong in a place like the Rusty Nail. I'm sure Olivia knows that. From what my brother's said she's a little quirky but not stupid."

"You're too damn judgmental."

"No, you wait 'til you've been working the field for fifteen years and you'll be saying the same thing." He tied the plastic bag with his clothing then tossed it at Matt. "It gets old after a while."

"Then why not quit?"

"Because I'm damn good at what I do."

Matt nodded as they strode out the exit, and on the way out, Ty thanked the nurse who'd given him the scrubs.

She gave him a coy smile in return, and as soon as they were outside, Matt gave him a smack in the gut.

"Susan has it bad for you."

Ty shook his head. "I'm not looking."

Matt glanced over his shoulder at the ER entry. "Why the hell not? She certainly doesn't strain the eyes."

"I'm not looking for a woman, period. No woman. I don't need the aggravation."

"You're just gun-shy after that last one, not that I blame you. She had you fooled—"

"Don't remind me." Ty climbed into the passenger seat and pulled a protein bar and mineral water out of his mini-cooler wedged as far under the dash as he could get it. "Not every guy gets lucky enough to find Miss Perfect when he's fresh out of college."

Matt started the truck's engine and smiled. "Well, if you're not looking, how will you know when you find Miss Perfect? Hell, she could by lying at your feet and you wouldn't know it."

"I'll know." He unscrewed the water's cap and washed down a mouthful of chewy bar with a couple of large gulps.

"She'll be the one with a refrigerator full of these, a body most women can only dream of having, and a heart as big as a Mack truck. How could I miss her?"

"It's easier than you think, pal. Trust me."

Chapter Two

"I want to do a good deed," Olivia said as she climbed into the taxi the following morning, exhausted after spending the better part of the night in the emergency room being poked and prodded by a merciless team of doctors, nurses and techs. "We both had a close call—"

"Thanks to you," Ann interrupted, touching the white bandage wrapped around her head. "It's official. You know I always thought you were a little wacky, but now I'm thinking they should have called in the guys with the white I-love-me coats with all the pretty buckles. Come to think of it, I must be no better than you, considering I let you talk me into staying in that pit for as long as I did."

"Well, who would've guessed they'd attack us like that? We were minding our own business. Where I grew up, the rule of the street was *live and let live*."

"I think it's more like *eat or be eaten*. Those guys could care less about us. And look at the result. The doctors shaved my hair off! I have a huge bald spot. And it could have been worse. I could be in a bed right now, in a coma. Not to mention the fact that my purse and keys are missing. Some...whatever you want to call those scumbags...knows who I am, where I live. That's downright frightening."

"I'm sorry. I really am." Olivia sighed then gave the driver directions back to her place. "Stay with me today. Tomorrow, you can call a locksmith and have the locks changed. I'm willing to bet your purse is at the bar, lying under a table or something. The place was a mess."

Ann gripped the door as the driver sped away from the hospital. "I hope my extra set of car keys are still at home...come to think of it, I hope my car's still in the parking lot. For all we know, it could be halfway to Mexico by now."

"No offense, Ann, but I doubt your '99 subcompact is a hot commodity."

"Hey, did you happen to notice the cars in that parking lot? I'd say the mean age of what few were there was about twenty years, and massive gas-guzzlers at that. I'm sure a guy on the run would appreciate a car that gets over ten miles to the gallon."

"I suppose you're right." Olivia tipped her head back, intent upon nursing her pounding headache until the driver made a quick right, throwing her across the bench seat. She bumped into Ann and chuckled. They both had to look pitiful, dark circles under their eyes, clothes tattered, heads bandaged.

"You find the strangest things funny." Ann crossed her arms over her chest and turned away, riding the rest of the way back to their apartment complex in silence.

Within minutes, the cab was parked in front of their building. Olivia paid the driver and thanked him then climbed from the car, helping a shaky Ann across the parking lot to the front door. Just as they reached it, an ambulance pulled up and parked. Nobody rushed out like Olivia would have expected.

"I wonder what's going on. That's the second time in twelve hours we've seen one of those. Doesn't look like they're in a big hurry, though."

Ann wobbled inside, shouting, "Who cares? One of them probably lives in the building."

"I've never seen an ambulance parked here." Olivia ran inside to unlock her door and help her friend inside. Once Ann was settled into her spare bed, she went to the window and peered through the blinds. Despite the kind of exhaustion that made her nauseous, she had to find out what was happening.

Finally, a man climbed out of the front of the vehicle. He had something tucked under his arm and was reading something else in his palm. As he approached the building's main entrance, which just happened to be next to her window, she realized it was the EMT who had taken care of her the previous night. She couldn't forget his name. It was Ty.

And then she realized something else. Last night's Ty—the one she'd vomited on—was *the* Ty. Her brother-in-law. Boy, did he look different!

Either she'd been blind before, or last night's near-death experience did unexpected—and wonderful—things for the guy's face. He was absolutely gorgeous, she realized suddenly. Why hadn't she noticed it before? "Well, helloooo, handsome. What happened to you the past couple of years? And what are you doing here now?"

Hoping he'd forgotten all about last night's gastrointestinal mishap, she scurried to the kitchen to look for a thank-you token, anything to give her a reason to open her door and talk to him. She found it in the form of a small chocolate cake she'd purchased for the party but hadn't opened. "Perfect!" Cake in hand, she lunged for the door and opened it. He was already down the hall, headed for…

Ann's door?

"Excuse me," she called out to his back, self-consciously tugging at her dress's creeping hem. It liked to rest up around her pelvis.

Had he been that bulky and wide before? And his ass…round, not flat. Just perfect.

He turned around and wearing a no-nonsense expression gave her a questioning look. "Yes?" His gaze dropped to her chest for a fraction of a second before returning to her face. A dusky rose shade tinted his cheeks and ears.

He was blushing?

"I'm Olivia. From last night? The bar. Eve's sister. You took me to the hospital…" she let her words trail off, suddenly feeling foolish. Blush or not, this guy wasn't interested in anything but whatever business had brought him to the building.

"Yes. Olivia. I'm glad to see you made it home safe and sound." As he stepped closer, the true width of his chest became more apparent, as did his staggering height and the unbelievable hue of his clear, blue eyes. He'd never seemed so big before. Of course, the only time she'd seen him was at the wedding. Did men really grow that much in such a short time? "I'm here to give something to your friend, Ann Watson. Is she home? We called the hospital and were informed you'd both been released."

"She's inside my place. Her purse..." Olivia's gaze dropped to his left arm, which was tightly gripping something against his side. "We think it was stolen..." She looked up, into his eyes and suddenly forgot what she was saying.

Those were the bluest eyes she'd ever seen. And his face was so striking, his nose narrow and straight, his cheeks, his chin. He had a dimple that winked at her every now and then. "Piece of cake?" She thrust the cake at his chest.

He lunged forward to catch it and something dropped to the floor. Olivia didn't bother looking to see what it was. For now, all she cared about was the way his fingertips felt brushing against hers.

It was almost...electric.

Her heart raced and she felt her face heating. "I...um...wanted to thank you in person for taking such good care of me and my friend."

"It's my job. Besides, you're family. Eve would have killed me if I hadn't given you first-class treatment." He released the cake, obviously assuming she still had a firm grip on it. Not a good assumption. She doubted she had a firm grip on anything at the moment.

She fought to regain its balance, since it had been half in her hands, half in his. "Well, you do it very well...er, your job, that is." The cake fell with a plop on the floor. "Damn!" Then feeling stupid for cussing, she glanced up as she squatted, pulling her dress down to cover a bit of her indecently exposed thigh.

"Sorry! I don't normally throw cake at people's feet. Did I get it on your shoes?" She glanced up. The motion of squatting with her head tipped back made her dizzy, and she wobbled, catching herself with a hand on the floor.

He stooped next to her, and she grabbed his knee to steady herself until the pounding in her skull stopped.

"I'm just glad to see everything turned out okay," he said in a low, husky voice.

"We'll be as good as new by tomorrow, if I can get the jackhammers to stop drilling through my head." She tried to lift the cake, which of course had landed frosting-side down. Chocolate cake and gooey frosting squished between her fingers. "Oh, yuck! What a mess."

Not seeming to mind the mess, he helped her gather the chocolate and pile it on the cardboard plate. "It was a very nice gesture. We don't often get a thank-you from our patients, family or not." He licked one of his fingers and smiled. "Very tasty. But I don't eat cake. Gotta keep an eye on my figure, you know." He pointed to his nonexistent belly.

I'd be glad to do that for you. She once again found herself breathless and staring into two deep, blue eyes. "How sad. You never get a thank you? You perform such a…vital…service."

"It's enough to know we did the best we could." He reached around her. "Speaking of services, I brought this."

A gift? For me? How sweet! "Oh, you shouldn't have." She finally looked down. Ann's purse. "Oh! Thank God! She'll be so happy to know you had it. She was scared silly some thug had gotten his hands on it."

He carefully held the strap between chocolate-coated fingertips. "I put her keys in there, too. At least, I believe they were hers."

"Did they have a flower key ring?"

"Yes."

She nodded. "Then you guessed right."

"I figured most of the regulars in that dump wouldn't be carrying a key ring like that."

"Good guess." One hand balancing the cake remains, she slid her arm through the purse strap, hooking it in her elbow. Their fingers touched again, and another zap of electricity shot through her body, producing a shudder.

A few pieces of cake fell to the floor again.

"Here, let me help you up." Without waiting for a response, he stood and hooked his arms under hers and pulled.

His messy hands, balled into fists, sat very near her breasts. Too near…no, not near enough. It would be all too easy to smear that delectable frosting all over her chest…would he lick it off?

She scrambled to get her feet firmly under herself, not in a particular hurry. With both hands covered in mess and out to her sides, her unsteady legs gave her the perfect excuse to lean against him.

What a body! Her soft form rested against firm, muscular bulk. Nope, she was in no hurry to regain her balance, or her composure. Not when the reward was so…heavenly. The funny thing was he didn't seem to mind it, either. He certainly wasn't shoving her away.

A sneak a peek at his face suggested quite the opposite. His face was not only red, but also strained.

And as her hip pushed against his pelvis, she realized something else was strained, too. Something long, and hard…and yummier than what coated her hands.

She smiled. "Do you want to come in?"

His eyes widened. "Come in where? Oh, I—"

What were you thinking, bad boy? If it's what I think you're thinking, I like you already. A lot. She tipped her head to the side. "To wash your hands."

"Oh! Sure! Thanks."

Grateful she'd left her apartment door slightly wedged open, she pushed it with her shoulder and stepped inside. She could feel him behind her. It was like a warmth heating her back.

"The kitchen's this way." She led him into the kitchen, dropped the cake in the overflowing trash, and set Ann's purse on the table, atop the board game from last night's get-together. Self-conscious because of the clutter, she pushed aside a handful of dirty bowls half-filled with uneaten snacks and turned on the sink, stepping to the side to let him wash first. "Sorry my place is such a mess. We had a little get-together last night, and I didn't have time to clean up." She licked some frosting from her fingertip as she watched him wash.

Yum. It was such a shame to waste perfectly good cake…and the opportunity to have some fun. His short sleeves were just short enough to show off bulking biceps and tight triceps. Even his forearms were developed. Long bands of sinew flexed and bunched as he reached for the soap.

She resisted the urge to stop him from washing the cake coating his hands down the drain. He moved very meticulously, scrubbing palms, fingers and backs of hands with her vegetable brush like he was about to undertake brain surgery.

Then he handed her the brush. "Thank you." His hands up in the air, he glanced around, and she guessed he was looking for a towel.

"Paper towels are over there." Her hands under the faucet, she motioned toward the end of the counter with a nod.

When he dried and she dried, they both stood mute. He looked uncomfortable, and she wondered what he was thinking.

He probably wanted to run. Surely he didn't find her attractive? Looking like a prisoner of war. Hair disheveled. Her clothing filthy. Her apartment a pigsty. No way. Couldn't be. Could it? Of course, there was no way of knowing if she didn't do something… *Seize the moment! Look at him. It's worth a shot.*

"I was just wondering…do you like Thai food?"

"Can't say. I've never tried it. My partner, Matt, eats it for lunch all the time and the stuff smells so… Oh, shi…shoot! Matt!

I forgot all about him. He's out in the ambulance." Long strides carried her handsome EMT hero toward the door.

Knowing the golden opportunity was rushing past her in a blaze of blue uniform, Olivia followed him. "How about dinner? You pick the restaurant."

As he reached the door, he spun around to face her and halted. His gaze tangled with hers for a heartbeat. "When?"

"Tomorrow night?"

"I pick the place?"

"Sure. I like any kind of food, almost."

"Okay. It's a deal. I'll pick you up at eight." With a nod, he left.

"Wait!" She lunged out the doorway, catching him before he left the building. "You aren't going to tell Eve, are you?"

"I wasn't going to, but I can." He nodded and flashed a stunner of a smile.

"Please don't. She'll make way more out of it than it is, take my word on that," she said, hanging onto the doorframe for support. The world was tipping up and down, up and down. She blinked, hoping that might still the motion. "I'll see you tomorrow then."

"Yes. Tomorrow. I'm looking forward to it."

"Me, too." Stifling the urge to let out a loud shout of victory, she watched him leave then staggered back to the bedroom to tell Ann the good news about the date…and her purse.

Chapter Three

Olivia forced herself to leave her hands at her sides, knowing that the self-conscious tugging on her skirt would only draw more attention to how short and snug it really was. She'd never been to such a posh restaurant. She was definitely out of her league. "I feel a little underdressed," she whispered more to herself than to anyone else.

"Would you like to leave? We can go somewhere else," Ty offered.

"Oh, no. It's very nice. You said this is your favorite. I don't want to ruin it for you. Besides, I like the atmosphere. It's very...dark."

Then the hostess, cute, blonde, and young, of course, approached. Stepping up to her podium, she looked down her nose at Olivia before scanning the list before her.

Olivia held her tongue for Ty's sake and pretended she hadn't noticed. Women could be such snobs. Young, old and in-between. *Yes, I'm wearing a miniskirt to your hoity-toity restaurant. If you were going on a date with this stud, you'd be wearing one too, wouldn't ya?*

The hostess turned her attention to Ty. "May I help you?" The young woman clearly preferred what she saw when looking at him over Olivia, not that Olivia could blame her. The hostess blinked several times—either trying to get his attention or wetting dried-out contact lenses—and leaned forward.

To his credit, Ty either didn't seem to notice or wasn't flattered by her flirting. "Wilcox. We have a reservation for eight o'clock."

"Wilcox? Let me see..." The blonde ran her manicured fingertip down the list. "Here you are. For two?" She glanced at Olivia again.

"Yes."

"Right this way. Your table is ready." Swaying narrow hips hugged by a knee-length pinstripe skirt, she led Ty and Olivia to a cozy table in the back of the restaurant. "Will this be okay?"

"Perfect. Thanks." Ty stepped around and pulled out a chair for Olivia and she sat.

"This place is very nice. And such service. Wow. We didn't have to wait a minute." Not sure what to talk about, and feeling more than a little tongue-tied, she watched him as he took his seat, unfolded his napkin and spread it over his lap, and carefully inspected his spoon. Either Mr. To-Die-For had worked in food service in the past or he was a little anal.

Mmm. She could fix that. Getting down and dirty was fun! Smiling at the thought, she picked up her menu and scanned the selection. Not a single vegetarian dish in sight. "Everything looks delicious," she lied. "Do you have any recommendations?"

"I always get a steak, steamed vegetables, and a tossed salad, but I've heard the chicken is excellent, too.

She wrinkled her nose. "Actually, I'm a vegetarian. Haven't eaten a hunk of meat since I went on a tour of a meat packing plant ten years ago. I'll just say it left a lasting impression."

He grinned. "Looks like we're on opposite sides of the food fence. I follow a low-carb diet and you live on them."

Not surprised, she chuckled. "All that fat and cholesterol will kill you someday."

"I need lots of protein to build muscle as I work out. And it keeps me lean."

That it does. I'd like to see exactly how lean. Her gaze fixed to his chest, clothed in a snug, black shirt, and took a sip of water. When she couldn't speak after a few extra-long seconds, she diverted her attention to the menu and continued to search for a dish that didn't have dead animal carcass as its main attraction.

"Even so, it's not the kind of diet you'd want to follow over a long period of time. It's not healthy. Someday, you'll have a wife and kids to think about. Don't you want nice, clear arteries so you can enjoy a long life with them?"

"What makes you so sure I want a family?"

She glanced up from her menu. "You don't?"

Looking quite adorable, he grinned as he polished his knife with the corner of his napkin. "I'm not in a big hurry to get married."

"Me, neither," she assured him. "Although I have a friend or two who met their husbands and joyfully pranced to the altar with them within a few months. So far they've done okay. Look at my sister and your brother. They've been married for almost two years now, and she's ecstatic. Did you ever hear how they met?"

He set his knife down and proceeded to polish his fork. "No. He didn't tell me."

"In a grocery store."

"I've never heard of anyone starting a lasting relationship in the grocery store."

"Yep. In the produce department. He was trying to pick a cantaloupe but didn't know how to tell whether it was ripe. Evidently, every time he picks one for himself it's all green inside."

"That sounds like Trey." He laughed, and she enjoyed what that brief moment of joy did to his features. His eyes glittered and fine lines fanned from their corners toward his temples. Two dimples sank into his cheeks on either side of his mouth. "Don't tell me she told him to squeeze her melons."

"Knowing Eve, I'm sure she did. The girl has no decency as you've probably noticed. We're nothing alike." She winked. "Anyway, as the story goes, they went home together that night and haven't spent a night apart since. It was love at first sight."

The waitress stepped up and took their drink and dinner orders.

Ty set down his hand-polished dinnerware and handed her his menu, then Olivia's. "You seem a little too worldly wise to believe in that kind of nonsense. I told him he was nuts for marrying her so soon."

"I'll be right back with your drinks." Clearly an intelligent woman who could take a cue, the waitress hurried away.

"Nonsense? Maybe I'm committing date suicide here, but we aren't exactly strangers are we?" When he shook his head she continued, "I wouldn't call love at first sight nonsense. Maybe it's a lofty ideal. An impossible dream. Something most people never experience. But I think it's real. Granted, I'm not holding my breath waiting for it, but I also won't close my eyes and ignore it if I happen to find it."

"So, you haven't found it yet?"

Lust, yes. Love? Well… She shook her head, knowing if she didn't, she'd send him running from her so fast she wouldn't know what had happened. Men did not like to hear about a woman's past loves. "Not yet," she said, trying to sound casual. The conversation was getting way too intense for her comfort, family or not. Suddenly parched, she sipped some iced water. "Wow, we've managed to knock out a couple of deep subjects already. Love and the hazard of eating red meat. Maybe we should try some small talk next."

He mirrored her, taking a few long swallows of water then licked away the clinging dampness from his upper lip.

Her gaze glued itself to that bit of ruddy flesh, and she wondered what he might taste like. Her insides hummed with energy. "I'll start," she said. "What happened to you at the wedding? You didn't stay for the reception."

"I was…um, called into work."

"That's awful! On the night of your brother's wedding?"

"Duty calls." He sighed and set his glass on the table. "I'm terrible at small talk. How about you tell me what you do for fun? Besides risking your life by going to bars frequented by ex-cons, that is."

"It is?"

"Don't tell me you couldn't tell."

The waitress returned with drinks and appetizers, asked if she could get them anything else then hurried off again.

Olivia watched her hasty retreat. "They have great service."

"That's why I like coming here." He held up his beer. "Shall we toast?"

She touched hers to his. "Sure."

"To getting to know each other, finally."

She nodded. "I'll drink to that." Then she sipped her margarita. Tangy. Tasty. She watched him take a swallow of his beer.

He licked his lips and she did the same. "Waiting for that answer."

Heck, yes! I'd love to go home with you…oh, that's not what he asked. "I do a lot of things for fun. Eve hasn't told you?"

"Honestly, I only see her during holidays. And those are chaotic. Otherwise, I'm usually busy with work."

"Sounds like you need to loosen up a bit, get some hobbies. I skydive, white water raft, am a certified hang gliding instructor. I've bungee jumped…"

"Ah, an adrenaline junkie."

"No. If you ask my friends and family, they'll tell you I'm just plain crazy."

"Now, I'm not surprised to have dragged you out of Rusty's. I've never even thought of trying anything riskier than going downtown—"

"Actually, isn't your work rather risky?"

"Maybe. But it's work. Not play. I've seen too many people get seriously injured doing things like you do, chasing a rush. I can't see how a moment of thrill would be worth risking your life—"

"It isn't. I don't believe I'm risking my life. A few limbs, maybe." She grinned to let him know she was joking and took another drink of her cocktail.

He smiled back. "You're quite a handful, aren't you?"

In an effort to flirt a little, she leaned forward, tipped her head slightly and pulled at the corner of her napkin. "Only if you're trying to hold me down."

Clearly sensing the vibe she was trying to send, he bit his lip and leaned closer to her. "I can't imagine anyone being foolish enough to think they could do that."

She stared into his eyes. "There are a few ways." Maybe he didn't care for jumping from high places, but he seemed to have a bit of adventuresome nature in his anal-flatware-polishing-safe-playing-hunky EMT self.

One brow rose. "Oh, really? How's that?"

The waitress stepped in just before she could go into that one. It was probably for the better. She wasn't sure how much he really wanted to hear. She felt compelled to be honest with him, but knew she could scare him away.

Slow down! This isn't a race. Enjoy the give and take… Oh, my God. She watched him pull an oyster into his mouth, the glimmer of butter clinging to his lips as they tilted into a devious grin. *Like hell, am I going to take this slow! Eve, you're going to be proud of me this time. Geronimo!*

"If you want to find out what it takes to hold me down," she cooed in her sexiest voice, "come home with me and I'll show you."

*****

She'd been practically under his nose for two years, and he'd never thought to look, despite Eve's nagging pleas to consider it. Of course, there had been one very good reason for him not to have taken notice of his sexy blonde sister-in-law before. Karen.

Funny thing was Olivia was nothing like Karen—or anyone else he'd dated for that matter. He preferred his women subdued, organized—which Olivia clearly was not. He sought a responsible woman with solid values and a good work ethic. Someone who shared his ideas about things.

Olivia seemed to be about as opposite him as a woman could be.

So why was he so damn intrigued? Not only did she mentally challenge him. She was witty. Her comebacks quick and lively. But she was also incredibly sexy. His cock was stiff as steel, and as they ate and their banter flowed, it only grew worse…or better, depending on how you looked at it.

God help him, he wanted to do exactly as she'd suggested. He wanted to come home with her and find out how much of tonight had been teasing and how much of it was genuine seduction. Thinking of the possibilities left him in agony.

He could throw her flat on her back on the bed and pin her luscious body under his. And fuck her until she couldn't move. Oh, yeah. That would probably work. He imagined her satisfied smile afterward and smiled himself.

"What are you grinning about?" she asked, interrupting his vivid daydream. She pushed her half-empty plate away. "I'm stuffed."

He glanced down at his, surprised to see that he hadn't eaten much at all. "Me, too." Sure he couldn't eat any more, he flagged down the waitress, requested boxes and the check then asked Olivia if she wanted some dessert.

She declined but hinted at something else she had in mind. She hurriedly grabbed the check and paid for supper as she had invited him out as a thank you.

He knew what kind of dessert she wanted, and it wasn't on the menu. He wasn't sure if he wouldn't simply throw himself at her feet when he dropped her off at home and beg her to make him her final course.

That scared him a little. No woman, not even Karen, had held that much power over him.

Boxes filled, check paid, he pulled out Olivia's chair and followed her out of the restaurant, his gaze resting on her lush, round rump. Damn, it was beautiful. The tight miniskirt she wore showed it off to perfection.

She grinned and brushed against him as he pushed open the front door for her, and she took advantage of another instant of nearness when he held the car door for her. She was no stranger to seduction, did it damn well.

As he drove her home, she slid her hand over his thigh and left it there. It didn't roam up. It didn't squeeze. It just sat there. But even that seemingly innocent touch was enough to overload his already strained nerves.

Speaking of strained, his undershorts were getting way too snug for comfort.

Either oblivious to the effect she was having on him, or pretending not to notice, she chattered about her sister, their family, and his brother as he drove the short distance to her house. Too nervous to talk, he tried to concentrate on getting her home in one piece. As he pulled into her driveway, he braced himself for what he expected her to ask him next.

She turned her body toward him and rested one palm on the dash. "You will come in, won't you?"

"I could, but—"

Her other hand slowly crept up his thigh. "I had a lot of fun tonight."

He swallowed. Hard. Blood pumped to his groin in angry, urgent bursts. "So did I."

"Do you have to work tomorrow?"

"Later. I'm working the midnight shift."

Her hand crept a little higher. "Then, you don't have to get up early tomorrow."

"Nope. So…" He paused, knowing what he wanted to do, but not sure if he should do it. Then her hand found its intended target and all doubt left him in a shudder. "You're going to show me how a guy holds you down, eh?"

She squeezed his cock through his pants. "Yep. I can see you're ready, willing, and hopefully able to face the challenge."

Chapter Four

If there was a single part of her that wasn't tingling, Olivia couldn't name it. Thanks to lively conversation, delicious food, and a man so sexy her panties were sopping, there wasn't a single cell in her body that wasn't tense, energized and waiting for release.

Play-it-safe or not, Ty did things to her no man had ever done. A slight glimmer in his eye made her heart jump into overdrive. A tiny lift in his voice made her shudder. A brushing touch made her pussy throb. Her whole body yearned to be close to him, as if any bit of space between them was too much.

And she wasn't afraid to show him exactly how she felt. Playing this dangerous game with him—a game of risk and seduction—was excruciatingly exciting. Never had she been so bold! But it was paying off in huge dividends.

Here they were, at her front door, and she knew what was going to happen next. He pressed his body against her back as she turned toward the door to unlock it, and instinctively her hips tilted back until her bottom was fitted snug against his arousal.

Oh! She rocked her hips and he groaned, bringing a satisfied smile to her lips. She had the feeling this would be the most intense, incredible, teeth-gnashing lovemaking of her life. It couldn't come too soon. "Here we are." Foam carryout box in one hand, she turned the doorknob and pushed open the door.

No sooner did she step inside than Ty's hands were exploring every part of her. Breasts, ass, face. Fingers tangled in her hair at the back of her head, tugging until she dropped her head back. His lips kissed her neck while tongue and teeth gave birth to shivers and goose bumps.

Overwhelmed, feeling ravished—and loving it—she spun around, reached out, gripped whatever part of him she could reach and held on as he back-stepped her until her spine was pressed against the wall. His knee wedged between her legs and feeling wanton, she rocked her hips back and forth, trying to rub away the throbbing ache.

Then he lifted his head, looked at her through glazed eyes and pressed his mouth to hers in a fierce kiss. No effort was made to hold back. His tongue lashed wildly in her mouth as his hands cupped her breasts and kneaded them. She returned his passion, dropping one hand between their bodies to find the swelling at the front of his pants and rubbed. He growled into her mouth, a welcome reward, then drew her tongue into his mouth and sucked it.

She felt the dampness of her arousal cooling her flaming pussy but it didn't help diminish it. She needed more. She needed his cock deep inside.

Breaking the kiss, she whispered, "Let's go to the bedroom, close the front door before the neighbors get out their video recorders."

Without speaking a word, he slammed the door and bolted it, took the food from her and set it on the console table next to the door, then swept her into his arms and carried her effortlessly down the hall. He stopped between the two bedroom doors. "Which one?"

"This one." She pointed at the last door, and he pushed open the door with a broad shoulder and carried her to the bed.

He didn't toss her, or drop her, or throw her like she'd half-expected. Instead, he lowered her softly, lovingly, while his gaze—aflame with passion—wandered over her face. "Are you sure?"

"Is there any part of me that seems to be saying otherwise?"

"No."

"Then take what you will!" She spread her arms wide open. "I'm yours to ravish. Or would you rather I give a little fight? I'm not giving you much of a challenge."

"Oh, yes, you are. I'm struggling to keep from ripping off those clothes and fucking you."

Her face flamed. "Good. I wouldn't want to make this too easy for you." Encouraged by his strained expression as he held himself over her by two very strong, very thick arms, she unfastened her shirt one button at a time. "Do you like black lace?"

His gaze slid down her throat to follow the widening, plunging V as she opened her blouse. He didn't speak, merely visibly swallowed, and she giggled.

"I'll take that as a yes." She unbuttoned the last one and peeled first one side of her top away then the other, shuddering as he licked his lips and lowered his head.

His tongue delved between her breasts, stopping at the tiny center bow between the two demi-cups. Then it wandered up high over the swelling of her right breast. Her back reflexively arched to push her chest higher and she yearned to pull the lace down to expose her nipple.

As it turned out, she didn't have to. Ty did it for her just before he pulled her nipple into his mouth and sucked hungrily. Shifting his weight back to free his hands, he dropped one to her other breast, pulling the lace down before pinching the nipple into aching erection. She reached down to try to rub his cock through his clothes, but he caught her wrists, his tongue still tracing hot circles over one nipple, then the other, and lifted both arms over her head. He held them there with one large hand and dropped his other one to her thigh.

Her legs parted and her pussy throbbed as she awaited his first touch. It wasn't gentle. She gasped as he hooked his fingers around the thin panel of lace covering her pussy and ripped it away. When he plunged those same fingers inside she shrieked with surprise and relief. Instinctively, she moved her hips in time with his thrusts, eager to find the relief of orgasm.

"Damn, you're wet."

She moved her legs further apart as her thighs and stomach bunched into tight coils. "More!"

He released her hands and slid to the end of the bed. With hands on her knees, he pressed them wider apart and up toward her chest, then parted her labia and dipped his head to taste her.

His tongue flickered over her throbbing clit quickly and her inner walls gripped his fingers. It was almost too much. Her head swam. Her blood burned her veins. Her nose pulled in the scents of his skin and her own arousal. Her tongue tasted of him.

Then, dizzy and nearly blind with need, she looked down and pushed his head away from her pussy. Between gasping breaths, she begged, "Please, no more."

"I want to see you come."

"I want you to feel me come."

He shook his head. "I won't last long."

"Neither will I." And then she hesitantly added as she quickly undressed. "Do you have a condom?"

"Yes." He nodded and produced one from his back pocket.

"Will you let me put it on you?"

He hesitated before answering. "Yes."

"I promise I won't torture you as long as you've tortured me." She first pulled off his well-fitting knit sweater, not surprised to find the hard, lean lines of a man who regularly pumped iron. His abs were tight, his chest broad and smooth, his skin was soft and velvety, void of any hair, anywhere. "You shave?"

"Sometimes."

"Everywhere?"

"I'll let you find that out for yourself." He motioned toward his zipper and a bolt of energy charged through her already overloaded body.

She quickly unzipped his pants and pulled them off, then drew in a deep breath and took hold of the wide elastic band of his snug boxer-briefs.

As she kneeled on the mattress and slowly slid them down to mid-thigh, releasing his thick cock, she felt the juices of her arousal dripping down her thigh. *Oh God!* Her gaze shot to his face. She found out...he did shave everywhere.

He grinned and she felt her eyes widening.

She'd always thought cocks—thick, long, huge—like that only belonged to men who either had surgery or were born with some rare genetic anomaly. "I...uh... Oh..." Her pussy clenched and unclenched around an emptiness that ached to be filled. Oh boy, would that tool fill it! She lowered her head and swirled her tongue around the smooth skin on the tip and felt his thigh muscles tense under her fingertips.

His groans of pleasure sent a wave of heat between her legs and the image of impaling herself on that glorious shaft made her shudder.

She opened her mouth wide and took as much of him in as she could—which admittedly wasn't much. To compensate, she gripped the shaft in her fist and working hand and mouth together, brought him to near climax, gauging from his moans and thrusts. When he stopped her by gripping her hair in his hands and pulling sharply, she slid on the rubber, pulled his boxers completely off and lay on her back. "Fuck me. Please. Now."

His face a mask of urgency, he climbed onto the mattress and held himself high above her on arms and legs. He wedged his knees between her legs and forced them apart and in one long thrust buried his thick cock deep inside.

She gasped at the pleasure of being filled. Waves of heat ripped through her before he even began moving. Sitting back on his knees, he changed angles. His cock glided in and out, raking against the sensitive inner walls until she wondered if she could take another moment. His hand dropped to her pussy and parted her lips. His fingertip traced quick circles over her clit.

Her inner walls tightened around his cock, increasing the sensation.

"Yes, baby. That's it. God, yes," he groaned, the sound only rocketing her closer to release. "Come for me. I want to feel you. Come for me now!"

She knew it was close and racing closer, yet she wanted to fight it. She wanted the fullness, the pleasure to last longer.

"Come now!" His thrusts came quicker, his voice hoarse with need. "Damn it! I want to fill you. You feel so good."

She consciously tightened her inner walls around him again, luxuriating in the increased fullness of his impending climax. His fingertips dug into her hips as he lifted them off the bed and held them for leverage. His cock pounded in and out without mercy, each time sending her hurling toward climax.

Her heart beat one final thump in her ear as the first spasm of climax shook her body, sending pulsing waves of hot agony out from her center. Her voice blended with his, rising into the air in a chorus of release just as her body melded with his in orgasm, both spasming, twitching, quaking, until both were shaking and spent.

After disposing of the condom, he lowered himself to the bed and cradled her to him, and she closed her eyes and enjoyed the simple ecstasy of being held and of the residual twitches and shivers of the orgasm of a lifetime.

When her breathing slowed enough to speak, she sighed. "Wow."

"Yeah," he said, his voice also a raspy whisper.

"I've never… I mean I have, but never like that. Oh, God." She tipped her head to glance up at his profile.

His lips pulled into a smile. Tiny beads of perspiration sparkled over his face, on his forehead and along his jaw. "Glad to hear it."

"What about you? I mean, it's probably weird talking like this right afterward. But I'd like to know."

"If it had been any better, you would have killed me."

"So, does that mean…?" She knew what she wanted to ask him, but also knew it could be taken wrong. The last thing she wanted to make him think was that she was needy. Most men didn't like needy women, at least not the kind that didn't have serious control issues, like her last boyfriend.

"What?" He turned his face toward hers.

"I…can't. It's silly. Nothing. Really."

His brows huddled low over his eyes. "We just had incredible sex, shared our bodies with each other and now you're afraid to ask me a simple question?"

"I'm not afraid."

"Well, then?"

Simple? Is it a simple question? "I wanted to know if that meant you'd like to do it again."

His brows shot to the top of his forehead. "Now?"

"Oh, not now." She giggled. "Although I wouldn't complain… I mean another time. Another date. Maybe next weekend sometime. That is, if you think…" She sighed and hid her eyes behind her hand. "Am I being too pushy? I do tend to be a little pushy, and when I'm nervous I also talk too much, too."

He reached across his chest and caught her chin in his hand. "Why are you nervous?"

She peeled her fingers away from her eyes. "Because of what we just did, and what I feel, and—"

He hoisted his shoulders up, bending an elbow and resting his head on his fist. "What do you feel? Tell me. I want to know."

"I'm scared... I mean, I don't want to scare you away."

"What makes you think you'll do that?"

Her gaze moved to the ceiling. She didn't want to read whatever was in his eyes, wasn't ready yet. It would probably be bad. It was always bad. Men didn't like clingy women who talked about love or commitment—or even second dates—too quickly. They liked strong, independent women who gave them a little bit of challenge. Men liked to chase women. Not have them fall into their laps. "Because I give too much away too early. There's no mystery to keep you coming back for more. I can't seem to help it. And since we're...well, family, I want to be honest with you, even if I am risking scaring you away. I have to be honest. If you want a good chase, you might as well forget it. I'm not a scared little rabbit. I don't test the waters and run away. And I don't play games. I close my eyes and dive right in."

"Are you saying...you're diving in...to me?"

She cringed at the shock she heard in his voice. "Maybe. Kinda. I know. Crazy, isn't it? I wish I could keep my mouth shut, but there's too much at stake here, even if we hardly ever see each other. You never know."

"Crazy? No. Just a little...risky." He caressed her shoulder. "I'm flattered—"

"But," she interrupted. "There's always a *but*. Let me guess. But you take things slow, and we don't know each other that well, and we should just take our time, and enjoy things as they come. Right?" She forced herself to look at his face and found a very sincere and gentle expression. Not a hint of panic shaded his eyes. That surprised her.

"Generally, that's a very good idea. Take things slow and enjoy learning about each other. But I have to admit, I'm teetering on the brink of diving in myself. I've never felt... I never..." He shook his head. "It makes no sense."

Encourage by his confession, she asked, "Does it have to? I don't think it's wrong to follow your heart sometimes. Don't you do that when you work? Follow your instinct when logic would suggest something else? Is it any different?"

"Yes, I do. Sometimes I know even though everything looks okay, something's wrong. I get a feeling."

"See? And you always do the right thing when you follow that instinct, am I right?"

"Pretty much."

She rolled onto her stomach and looked into his eyes. "What's your instinct telling you now, Ty?"

He closed his eyes, and breathless, closed off, she waited for his answer, knowing she'd either blown it right then and there and he'd run for the hills and never return. Or…or! What if he did see things her way? Could they be on the brink of rushing into a crazy, whirlwind romance like her sister and his brother had? The kind of relationship she'd always dreamed of having. The kind that took on a life of its own, grabbed her around the neck, and pulled her into it.

The thought sent a ripple of excitement through her body. For some reason, this unlikely man—with a suspected bundle of anal-retentive habits—was absolutely fascinating. She couldn't wait to explore his mind, body, and soul. That would be so much easier if he could lower his defenses, at least a little.

He licked his lips, a telltale sign he was about to speak. "My instinct is telling me you're a beautiful, adventuresome, intelligent woman who would jump into a raging fire to save a kitten. I want to know you. I've wasted a lot of time."

She smiled. That sounded promising.

"But I will not allow either of us to rush into anything. I've learned that's a big mistake. I get the feeling there are a lot of differences between us. There's no way we'll do like my brother and your sister did, get married mere weeks after meeting."

"We met two years ago," she pointed out to him, just in case he'd forgotten.

He nodded. "True."

"See there? We've known each other a long time." She raised herself on hands and knees, lifting her right arm and leg to straddle on top of him. "I won't pressure you... I mean, I won't pressure you any more than I have." She lowered her hips until her pussy rested on his flaccid cock. It twitched against her skin.

He gripped her hips and held them still. "What makes you think this—we—are so right? Already?"

She grinned and shrugged. "Like I said, I feel it." Sensing he was uncomfortable, she lifted herself off his pelvis and sat next to him, drawing the sheet up to cover herself from the waist down. "Sometimes you lose if you don't listen to that inner voice. You lose opportunity—or more. Look at my work. My sister told you what I do, didn't she?"

"Stocks?"

"Yes. I'm a day trader. Many times I act on a hunch—a gut instinct. Sometimes I second-guess myself and hesitate. Every time I've done that I wished I had just gone with my initial feeling. Each of those instances has cost me thousands of dollars. I've learned to quickly weigh risk and make decisions. My entire future is based on my ability to do so."

"I don't know how you live like that. My job might be stressful, but I know where my paycheck comes from every week. I need some things to be stable."

"It's not for everyone but it works for me. The pressure of knowing I have to succeed keeps me going. I love my work. I love the highs and lows and everything in between, couldn't go back to working for some corporation punching a clock and drawing a weekly paycheck if my life depended on it."

"But does every aspect of your life have to involve that kind of risk-taking? Isn't there any part of you that craves stability?"

She sat back against the headboard and thought about it, trying hard to think of an area of her life where stability was essential. For the most part, she drew a blank. She didn't care if she lived one day in Detroit and the next in Chicago, or Seattle, or Paris. She didn't care if she walked, rode a bus, or drove her car. A job was not a priority. But maybe love. A safe, stable romance with a man who wouldn't stray sounded wonderful. Would he want to hear that? Probably not yet. Then again, maybe. "Just the basics, I suppose. I need a semi-steady heart rate, my computer, and a reliable Internet hookup. And…well, in personal relationships, too. Stable…er, friendships."

He looked adequately surprised, clearly getting what kind of friendships she meant. "And yet, you're willing to rush into something that may or may not work out?"

"Sounds illogical, doesn't it?" she admitted. "Irrational and impulsive. I know." She stood, dressed and searched for her purse, watching him watch her. He looked so amazing reclined in bed, the sheet pulled up to just above hip level, allowing her a spectacular view of scrunched up abs. His face was still flushed. "I don't think real rationally after sex. I'm probably talking in circles, or worse. Sorry." She swallowed an attempt to make any more excuses for the strange conversation. He was a man. He couldn't understand. Most men understood sex but not much about deeper feelings. Hell, she was having a hard time understanding herself at the moment. While she prized a solid, steadfast relationship, she wasn't willing to be patient and let things happen on their own. She had to push.

That had to be it. She was—gasp!—impatient. Or worse, a control freak. What a surprise…not. How many times had she been called both?

"Can you do me a favor?" She sat on the edge of the bed and reached for his hand. His large one closed firm and warm around hers and she smiled. "Can you please develop a sudden case of amnesia? I'd be mighty grateful. I'd say from right about the time we both sighed after that amazing fuck. Just forget about everything after that point. Okay?"

He grinned and for a brief instant she considered hopping back into bed with him and going for round two. But she resisted. She needed some time to think. Some time to cool off.

She needed to give him some space, too.

He tipped his head slightly, the angle giving his face a playful, boyish quality. "Are you going somewhere?"

"Yes, I think I should leave now. I...uh..." She glanced around the room, suddenly realizing exactly why he was looking so puzzled and amused at the same time. She was in her bedroom. In her apartment.

How had she become so brain-dead?

He pulled the sheet aside and stood, seemingly unaware of exactly how beautiful his unclothed body was. Every part, from head down, was sculpted perfectly. Every line and angle. Every dip and curve.

He bent down to gather his clothes and sat to redress. "I think it's time I go home. I'm helping a friend move tomorrow morning. I should get at least a couple hours sleep before then. He has a piano that weighs a ton."

"Sounds painful." Her brain mired in confusing thoughts, she watched him hide his gorgeous physique under a pair of pants and his clingy knit pullover sweater then walked him to the front door and watched him sit and put on his shoes and socks. When he was finally dressed, she took hold of the doorknob but didn't pull it open. "Thank you for tonight. It was..." She felt her cheeks heating and lifted a hand to cover one side of her face. "I mean, I had a great time. And thanks for the delicious dinner. Oh! I should put those in the refrigerator." She motioned toward the boxes still sitting where he'd set them. "I can have the leftovers for lunch tomorrow."

"I had a great time too. Goodnight." He lowered his head to kiss her, and she closed her eyes, pursed her lips and locked her knees in expectation.

His kiss, soft and tender but a little reserved, was nice, but it wasn't what she had hoped for. Not to mention it ended much too soon, which left her feeling cheated and a little empty. Still, she smiled and opened the door for him.

"Goodnight," she whispered as he walked past her and out the door. "Sweet dreams."

"Goodnight, Olivia." He didn't promise to call, nor did he mention a future date. He just left.

Once he was out of sight, she closed her door, put the remains of her dinner away and went back to bed, hoping she'd feel better about things in the morning. Thanks to her inability to play the cool mystery woman, and her reckless way of life, she was pretty sure that would be the last time she'd see the handsome, play-it-safe EMT, Ty. At least, outside of a future holiday party with family, or a medical emergency.

A shame.

Chapter Five

"You're quieter than normal today. What's up?" Matt asked, as he and Ty loaded the ambulance for their shift. After packing a few final essentials, he assessed Ty with sharp, trained eyes.

Ty shrugged, wanting to avoid the inquisition he knew would come next. "I had a late night. Watched the game—"

"Oh, yeah! The game my ass. You had a date with the fox from Rusty's. Did you think I'd forget? How'd it go?"

"Okay. But I don't think I'll be seeing her again." Ty rested a foot on the ambulance's bumper and leaned into his bent knee. "She's not right for me. No reason to drag it on. You know how women can get."

Matt slammed the back door closed then sat next to Ty's foot. "Why's that? Don't tell me she was a prude."

"Hell—I mean, no. She's no prude, by any stretch." Mosquitoes feasted on him, dive-bombing from all directions. Ty swatted first one arm, then the other. *Damn bugs.*

"Sounds perfect." Matt gave him a wolfish grin. The guy could be so shallow sometimes. "So, what's the problem?"

Another pesky bloodsucker buzzed in Ty's ear and he shook his head. "She's too…unstable. And she moves way too fast."

"In what way?"

"In all ways. No sooner did we…well, you know…than she was asking where we were headed…more or less."

"And you complained about the last one's games, how she left you guessing where you stood for months. I don't know about you, Ty. What the hell do you want?" Shaking his head, and Ty knew it wasn't because there was a bug trying to climb inside his ear, Matt stood and walked around the side of the ambulance. They both took their usual places, Matt behind the wheel, Ty in the passenger seat. "You broke up with Mary Poppins—"

"Karen. Her name was Karen." Ty scratched at the new welt on his forearm. "The mosquitoes are out for blood tonight."

"Quit scratching. You'll get an infection." Matt started the engine then looked in the mirrors and side to side before pulling into traffic. "Whatever her name was, she was a prissy schoolmarm who'd read too many how-to-trap-a-man rule books. You were miserable with her. It was pathetic."

"I wasn't miserable. I was just..." *What*? What had led him to break up with her? He remembered the sad excuses he'd told her. But they'd been empty, with no real substance. Truth was, he hadn't been honest with her, or himself.

"You wanna know what I think?" Matt glanced at Ty then returned his focus to the road.

"You're going to tell me no matter what I say, so go ahead. In fact, I'm curious."

Matt smacked the steering wheel. "I can't believe I just heard that. Maybe there's hope for you yet. It's about time you started listening to me."

"I didn't say I'd follow your advice. I'd be an idiot to do that. Your personal life is a circus."

Matt enjoyed a long guffaw. "You're jealous. I think you should give a high-wire act or two a try." He stopped at a light and grinned at Ty. "I think you need excitement from a woman, maybe more than I do. Your perfect woman is the opposite of what you think. She's wild, unfettered, a risk-taker. Ms. Perfect-for-Ty bungee jumps and skydives but she doesn't play games. She knows what she wants and she goes for it. She doesn't string any man along. And let's not forget the best part. In bed, she's an animal." He belted out, "Born to be wi-i-i-ild!"

"You're wrong. Opposites might attract in the short-term, but they don't work for long-term relationships."

"Who says? I know plenty who have. You're just scared I'm right. Chicken!" Mark let out a round of clucks.

Ty merely shook his head. "I'm not chicken. I'm being practical minded."

"See, that's your problem right there. You need to quit using the gray matter. Start feeling. Follow your gut."

Sounds familiar. He stared out the passenger side window into the darkness, watching houses drift by as they drove through a residential neighborhood.

A call came over the radio. A woman unconscious at an address on Beech Street, Olivia's street. Images of Olivia lying unconscious on the floor, her face pale, her golden hair stained red and fanned out around her head played through his mind. Shaking the thought away, he scribbled the address, scooped up the radio and responded as Matt flipped on the lights and sirens and headed south along Route Ten.

They stopped two houses shy of Olivia's apartment building and a huge sigh of relief huffed from his lungs. Then, he shifted into rescue mode, gathered his gear from the back and rushed toward the front door.

An elderly man, stooped, pale and dressed in only boxers and an undershirt opened the door. "She's this way." He motioned toward the hallway. "We were about to have a little snack and go to bed, and she was…dressing and then she just crumpled to the floor."

Ty knelt next to the woman, clothed in a black silk nightgown. "What's your wife's name? How old is she? Does she have any health problems?" He quickly assessed her breathing, pulse, and blood pressure.

"Erma. Seventy-three. She's diabetic."

"Anything else?"

"Not that I know of," the man said, sounding worried. "She's my life. Tell me she'll be okay. We've been married since we graduated from high school. I can't live without her."

"Sir, I'm doing everything I can." Ty dug through his supplies and did a quick sugar level. Just as he expected. Low. Very low. "When was the last time she ate?" He tied a tourniquet around her upper arm and felt for a vein.

"This afternoon. It's our anniversary. I wanted to take her out for dinner, have a nice quiet evening. She wanted to go somewhere else. Somewhere special. She insisted. It's tough to deny her anything." He shook his head. "Some of the best times I've ever had were when we did what she wanted, including tonight. But it wasn't worth this."

Ty, starting an IV, nodded. "I know what you mean. We'll give her some sugar, and hopefully she'll come around. But her level was very low." Matt handed him the syringe full of concentrated dextrose solution and he injected it into the port on her IV. They lifted her onto the backboard and then lifted the board onto the stretcher. As Matt secured her to the stretcher, Ty turned to the man. "We'll take her to St. Joseph's. Do you have a friend or neighbor who can drive you there? I'd take you with us, but I'm sure you'd like to dress first."

The man nodded. "I'll get there. Just take good care of my sweetie. She's everything to me, makes me a better man. I'd be a lifeless old coot if it wasn't for her."

"I'll do what I can, sir." Ty kneeled and gathered his equipment.

"You know how it is, don't you?" The man patted his shoulder.

"Sir?" He glanced up.

"To find the one person who fills all your holes. It took you by surprise, didn't it? She wasn't what you were expecting."

Not sure how to answer, because he wasn't sure how he felt, he simply said, "No."

"I knew it! You're in for a lot of surprises, young man. Enjoy every one of them. Now, before you're too old."

"Will do." The last of his equipment in hand, he stood and headed toward the door. "Good luck to you and your wife. We'll take good care of her."

"Thank you." The man smiled, displaying a toothless but worried grin as he followed. He patted Ty's arm. "You're a good man. I trust you."

Ty nodded and ran to the truck, helping Matt load the stretcher before climbing inside and giving him the signal when he was ready to go. The woman, clearly having made a quick recovery thanks to the sugar boost, gave him a playful smile.

He checked her blood pressure, heart and respirations then asked, "Hi, Erma, how are you feeling now?"

"Much better. Aren't you a handsome man?" She reached a shaking arm up to wrap cool fingers around his biceps. "Silly me. I should have eaten. But I didn't want to go up in that helicopter with a full stomach."

"Helicopter?"

"It was fabulous! George wasn't too crazy about the idea when I mentioned it. Has to take a Valium just to climb onto a stepladder. But once we were in the air, he loved it. It's our anniversary. We've been married fifty-two years."

"He told me." Ty did a second sugar level check. Much better.

"We were such an unlikely couple. So very different, right from the start. But we balance each other so well. George stabilizes me. He's a good man."

Ty nodded. "He was very worried about you."

"I'm sorry I made him worry." She frowned. "I make him worry a lot but he never complains. The man has lived through heart attacks. Strokes. He's a walking miracle. I think he needs a reason to fight. It's sad, but I think he stays alive just to make sure I'm okay."

The truck stopped in front of St. Joe's and Ty climbed out, following the gurney into the ER, reciting Erma's last blood pressure, heart rate and sugar level. As he left, both George and Erma's voices echoed in his head.

"She's my life."

"He stays alive just to make sure I'm okay."

Maybe there was something to the whole opposites-attract thing after all. Maybe he'd been wrong about what kind of woman he needed in his life. He knew deep inside he wanted to find out. His every thought revolved around one woman, an unlikely woman who spoke her mind and followed her instinct. He couldn't deny it. There was a bond there. Something that kept pulling him to her.

There was only one way to know for sure what might happen.

Was he willing to take such a huge risk with his heart?

And what would Olivia think? Would she trust him? She was no dummy. After what he'd said last night, a complete turnaround would be about as believable as the latest superhero movie.

He'd have to prove it to her, somehow. Maybe a chat with her friend would yield an idea or two.

*****

If this doesn't work, I'll be dying in vain. Ty swallowed hard, several times, and inched closer to the ultralight plane that would launch him into the air. That tiny thing, attached to the hang glider by a single rope, couldn't be strong enough to do the job. It looked like a toy. *What am I doing here? Will it prove what I want it to? It better!*

Olivia, busy with final preparations to the hang gliding equipment, didn't look up as she asked, "Are you all right?"

"Oh, yeah," he answered, forcing a casual tone to his voice to hide the fear. He didn't need her to know exactly how panic-stricken he really was. If she sensed it, she might offer him an opportunity to back out. And as the wind picked up, sending the sound of the meadow's overgrown ruffled grasses through the air, backing out was too damn tempting to turn down at the moment. "I'm…fine."

She glanced up and grinned at him. "Don't take this wrong, but when you called and told me what you wanted to do, I thought you were joking." She tipped her head and studied his face with sharp eyes. "I'm still not sure if you're serious, but you seem to be."

"Oh, believe me, I would never joke about something like this. I'm completely serious."

"Despite all the talk about danger and adrenaline junkies? What was it you said last weekend?" She tapped her temple with a slender finger. "Wasn't it something about not doing anything riskier than going downtown?"

"True. But our conversation got me curious so I did some reading. Hang gliding isn't as risky as I thought. Heck, seventy-year-old men do it."

"It isn't exactly a walk in the park," she challenged, giving him a playful smile. She reached for him and pulled him closer, and he stiffened against the urge to wrap his arms around her and kiss her until she'd forgotten all about gliders and planes.

After all, there was more than one way to get his point across, wasn't there?

"You aren't trying to talk me out of this, are you?" Instead of kissing her to oblivion, an option that sounded much sweeter to him, he forced himself to stick with Plan A, the crazy one, and followed her lead as she back-stepped, pulling him closer to the glider.

"Absolutely not!" A wicked glint sparkled in her eye. "Why would I do that? You'll be a good boy and let me strap you up, won't you?"

"You bet I will. I don't want to risk falling off." He followed her instructions as she fastened him to the glider, then fastened herself in next to him.

Finally, seeming to be pleased with herself, she glanced at Ann, who was standing by the car, and gave her a thumbs-up and then motioned to the ultralight's pilot. "Well, everything's ready. Let's get going, I can't wait! I think you're going to love it."

"Me, too." He swallowed several more times when his lungs refused to inflate, and gripped the bar in front of him until his forearms ached. The slack rope attached to the front of the glider pulled tight as the ultralight took flight. He closed his eyes and held his breath as they rolled down the short runway.

And then he felt his stomach flip, like it did when he was a kid and his father drove their truck too fast over the crest of a hill.

"You're missing it. You didn't pay all that money to keep your eyes closed, did you?"

"No, I'm just...enjoying the other sensations," he said, suddenly aware of the feel of soaring through the air and the wind buzzing in his ears.

"What do you think so far?"

"I'm not sure what to think, to be honest."

"The ultralight will be cutting us loose soon. We're almost at two thousand feet. Do you want to steer? Ty?"

He opened his eyes, and braced himself for the physical discomforts of panic. But, to his surprise, they didn't come. He smiled with relief, elation, and turned his head toward Olivia. "Me, steer? Oh, no. I trust you. You're the pro. I just want to enjoy the ride." He glanced around, at the wispy clouds high up above, and the meadow far below. Ann looked like an ant. "Wow, this is...great."

"Are you surprised?"

"Yes, very. I didn't expect to enjoy it... I mean so much." He watched as the ultralight released them and the buzz of the motor faded away as it descended toward the runway below.

"So, are you going to tell me why we're here?" she asked, her voice cutting through the soft whoosh of the wind, the only sound he heard outside of the pounding of his racing heart.

"Isn't it obvious?"

"No." She studied him and he tried to smile. "Now, fess up. If someone had told me I'd be up here today...with you, I would have laughed in their face. What's going on?"

"Wouldn't it be better to talk about this later? Like when we're back on solid ground?"

"And miss this opportunity? Heck, no!" She pointed at his chest. "Thanks to those straps, and roughly fifteen hundred feet of air between us and the ground, you're not going anywhere for a while."

It was no use. Not only couldn't he hide anything from her, clearly she possessed a woman's keen intuition, not that he was surprised. Among her more admirable features—and she had plenty—he found her sharp mind one of her best. But he also couldn't delay the conversation he knew was coming for another minute.

"It's part of our game," he admitted.

"*Our* game? What game? I didn't know we were playing a game. I mean, I was playing a silly game the other night with the girls. Did Eve tell you about that? I'm going to have to—" She steered the glider into a wide circle over a small cluster of trees.

"No, she didn't tell me about anything, but I'm curious. You'll have to tell me about that one later. I'm calling our game...Risk. Um, shouldn't we go that way, toward the field?"

"I'm steering. You're riding. Remember? Risk? Wasn't that a military board game of some kind?"

"Yeah, but this one's different. Do you wanna play it with me?" he asked, watching the trees get larger as they descended. It would hurt landing there. Pain was not one of his favorite sensations.

Looking far too relaxed, she continued to steer the glider farther away from the field. “I’m intrigued, but I have to know one thing first. What are the rules?”

“Well, there’s only one, really. You have to be open to taking chances—do the kinds of things you’d never dreamed of doing.”

“Well, considering our last conversation, I’d say I’m a lot more willing to do that than you are.”

Turn this thing around! “We’ll see about that.”

She turned her head and raised a dainty blonde brow. “Are you…challenging me?”

Turn it around now, before those tree limbs are scraping our bellies. “You could say that.”

“You’re on, buddy! Give me your best shot. I’ll face anything. But first, you’re going to face a few risks of your own…at my hands.” She grinned, pulled the bar closer, and the glider sped up, circling round and round, faster and faster.

Adrenaline slammed his nervous system, sending his heartbeat into an erratic gallop. He flushed, gasped, and howled in ecstatic glee as the glider carried him soundlessly over the top of the trees and toward the ground, which was nearing him at a breakneck speed. And just as it leapt upward and threatened to slam, he winced and closed his eyes in preparation for the impact.

Surprisingly, the glider landed smoothly and rolled to a stop.

He turned to look at Olivia, who gave him a mischievous grin.

“You enjoyed that, didn’t you?”

“You bet I did. But not as much as I’m going to enjoy what’s coming next.”

She gave him a coy smile as she unstrapped herself. “That sounds like a promise.”

He returned it with a flirtatious wink as she unfastened his harness, giving it one final tug before releasing him. "Call it what you will." He caught her arm and dragged her body against his, dropping his head to kiss her.

Her body molded to his as her mouth opened to receive his tongue. He took his time tasting her, enjoying the heady combination of arousal and adrenaline pumping through his body. His cock burned with the need to be inside her, and his hands dropped to squeeze her bottom.

She dropped her head back and gasped, murmuring, "A game called Risk is right up my alley. I can't wait!" Then she ground her hips into his pelvis and nearly brought him to his knees.

Chapter Six

Olivia barely made it in the house with her clothes on. Ty, wide-eyed and flush-faced and looking very alive, almost predatory, practically ripped her clothes off the minute they stepped inside her apartment. First, came her shirt, thankfully an old T-shirt she didn't care much about. Then, her shoes and socks. Finally, he kneeled at her feet and yanked her jeans down her legs before pulling her to the floor.

A surprised giggle escaped her mouth, but cut off when he forced her onto her back and held himself on hands and knees above. His breath warmed her face in quick puffs, and in his eyes she read such urgent desire her body instantly reacted. She tingled from head to toe.

"I feel so…alive," he murmured just before dropping his head to trail soft kisses down one side of her neck. A stream of air tickled her ear. "You've given me something I never expected, something I didn't know I was missing. I want to show you exactly how grateful I am for that."

She shivered and goose bumps showered her upper body. "Believe me, you're well on your way to doing that." Warmth flooded her groin and she tipped her pelvis up, eager to rub away the growing ache.

"I want to do so many things with you. So many crazy, wonderful things." He laughed. "I can't believe I'm saying this. I can't believe what I've done today. But I have no regrets. I've never felt like this before."

"Adrenaline has a way of becoming addictive." She reached up, looped her arms around his neck and pulled until his mouth fell upon hers.

His kiss was as wild as the look in his eye had been. Frenzied and uninhibited, and she met each hungry thrust of his tongue with one of her own. He groaned into her mouth, the sound echoing in her head and carrying through the rest of her body until she moaned in response. His weight settled on top of hers and she rocked her hips up and down, thankful for the friction.

Her blood flamed inside, setting mini-blazes throughout her body. Her senses came alive as every minute scent and sound amplified. It was as though each of his panting breaths raged through her body. The scent of man and arousal filled the air around her, and she closed her eyes and languished in the passion building inside her.

He broke the kiss, leaving her mouth and face tingling, and sat up. "It's more than that, you know. More than adrenaline. I want you to know that."

"Mmmm," was all she could manage to say. Although his mouth had stopped invading hers, his hands were roaming freely over her body. Squeezing, caressing. He unfastened the front clasp of her bra and held one breast in each hand, pulling on the nipples until she cried out.

"It's you. I know this is crazy. I know what you probably think. But… I need you in my life, and I think you need me. We're a perfect fit."

"In more ways than one." She reached between their bodies and cupped his erection through his pants. "Make love to me."

His body trembled over hers, and her heart raced at his obvious loss of control. "Promise me you'll take a chance with me. It might not be this way always, but I want to try. I can't stop thinking about you. I want to take care of you. And live life with you. Experience everything I can with you." He stopped touching her and her eyelids lifted.

He looked so tortured. Stress pulled at his face, neck and shoulders. It was visible in hard lines of tight muscle. "Promise me. I need to hear you say the words."

Her eyes burned and she blinked. “You’re not afraid? Just like that? Every doubt is gone?”

“I’d be lying if I told you all my doubts are gone, but that doesn’t mean I don’t want this. I do. I want to take a chance…on you, on life…on love. I haven’t changed. I doubt I ever will, but I see something now. I need balance. I need you, Olivia. And you need me.”

She blinked away some tears and pulled him to her, sighing as his weight rested heavily on top of her. “I promise.”

Several heartbeats pounded in her ears as she closed her eyes and drew in warmth and energy from him until she thought she might burst from an overload.

He sat up, undressed and knelt between her knees. She watched him, eagerly awaiting the fullness of his first thrust. He quickly pulled a condom from his pocket and rolled it on, then pushed her knees wider and teased her slit with the head of his cock.

White heat pooled between her legs and her thighs trembled. She reached overhead to brace herself against anything she could find. Her fingertips touched nothing but the carpet.

His hands rested on each of her knees and his cock pushed slowly, inch by delectable inch, into her pussy until she nearly wept. Then he pulled it out and slowly slid it back in, over and over. It was torture. With each thrust her entire body shook. Her heart pounded in her head. Her lungs drew in one ragged breath. The warmth of her impending climax slowly wound through her body, creeping higher and higher. She moaned. “Oh, yes!”

He stopped.

She gasped. “No! Not now.”

“Exactly. I want this to last.”

“I’m so close.” She tightened the inside walls of her pussy around his cock and then groaned as he pulled out completely. “You…meanie!”

"I want to see your ass." He eased her onto her stomach and then tickled the small of her back with his tongue. "Damn, what an ass." He pulled her cheeks apart and her back arched like a cat's. He whispered, "I want to fuck it. Will you let me?"

"With that huge cock? Oh..." She cringed against imagined pain.

He pulled her hips up until she was on her knees. "The couch. Over here."

She crawled to the couch and rested her chest on the cushions. Behind her, he pulled her knees wide apart and stroked her pussy with his fingers, thrusting several in and out of her pussy until her legs became weak. "Oh, God!"

"That's the way. Do you have any lube?"

"Nightstand," she grunted.

"Here." He caught her hand, pried her fingers from around the edge of the cushion and pulled it under her body until she was touching her pussy. "Touch yourself. I'll be right back. Don't stop."

She nodded and drew slow, lazy circles over her clit, sighing at the waves of warmth washing over her.

He returned within seconds. "Damn, what a sight!"

"I want you...inside me."

"In a minute. I'm enjoying this." He pulled her ass cheeks apart. "Fuck yourself with your fingers. Will you do that for me?"

She slid her left hand down her body and pushed them inside her pussy as her right hand continued to work over her clit. Overcome, she bit the cushion to keep from howling.

"I'm going to touch you now."

His finger, slick and wet, pushed at her anus and she repeated in her head, *Relax, relax*.

"Yes, just like that." A finger breeched the entry and pushed deeper inside, and she gasped and slowed the pace of her own hands, certain she would come if she didn't stop. "How does that feel?" he murmured.

"Won…der…ful… Oh…" She bit the couch cushion again.

His finger slipped out and the broad head of his cock took its place, sliding up and down her crack before pushing at her tight hole. Her anus burned and her back arched.

She bit back a cry. "Oh, no!"

"Remember our game? It's your turn now. Do you trust me? Take me inside." He kneaded her ass cheeks, as he continued pushing at her anus. "Take a chance and reap your reward."

Her pussy throbbed and her body soared toward completion, despite the burn, or maybe because of it. Pain and pleasure melded into one as every part of her shook and trembled and finally relinquished.

His cock pushed deeper and deeper and he howled.

Her cries joined his as her pussy started pulsing around her fingers, soaking them with the juices of her orgasm. Her ass pulsed around his still cock, milking it as it swelled.

He pulled out of her ass, then thrust deep inside one last time before finding his own release. His fingertips dug deep into the flesh of her thighs as he came, the sting only another welcome sensation.

And then the wild waves of pleasure eased to steady twitches and he pulled out, leaving her feeling weak and empty and sated.

No longer able to hold herself up, she let her bottom fall to the floor and rested against the couch. Her breathing slowed. Her pounding heartbeat left her head, settling back in her chest where it belonged.

And his warmth pressed against her back. "Come here." He pulled on her shoulders until she turned to face him. He gathered her into an embrace as he fell to the floor. His eyes searched her face as his fingers traced the line of her temple and jaw. "Thank you. Thank you for trusting me. For taking a chance with me. For showing me what I would have been missing. I won't ever take you for granted. I promise. Together, we can make every day a celebration. Every moment will count."

She sighed and nestled her cheek against his chest, grateful for the steady thump of his heart, and knowing she'd found her perfect match. Such an unlikely man, but so perfect for her. They would fill a gap in each other, like two linking puzzle pieces.

To think it had all begun with one game and it would continue with another.

They would both win as they played their game of risk.

That was all she'd ever wanted.

Enjoy this excerpt from

Lessons in Lust Major

Not again! Every time I'm summoned to this room, I end up regretting it for months. Kate Evans pressed her back against the interior brick wall, knowing the stooped, eighty-something year-old woman standing in front of her was no more pliant. If only Sister Joy Margaret wasn't the principle, the woman who held her future between her bent, arthritic fingers. Then again, next fall, Sister Joy would be retired. Unfortunately, Kate wasn't sure if that was a good thing or not. If nothing else, the little, quick-witted woman was predictably unpredictable.

Which was the main reason for Kate's currently miserable state.

The principle gave her wimple-covered head a firm shake. "Good! I'm glad you came so quickly. Mr. Krupke," her pale gray eyes twinkled as she said his name, "will be here in just a moment, and then we'll go over the details of your trip this weekend. I had to take some money from the art department's budget to send both the instrumental and vocal teachers to the conference, so I'm asking for some small concessions. Sister Mary Martha wasn't happy to lose the money."

I bet she wasn't. Concessions? How small? She swallowed a sigh, and turned her head when Sister Joy's office door creaked. But when Lukas Krupke, the school's new band instructor, didn't enter the closet-sized room as she expected, Kate looked at Sister Joy.

"As you know, this is the first year we've been able to afford sending both…"

Oh, boy, here it comes! Knowing whatever the principle had to say would be bad, she dug her fingers into the mortar between the bricks behind her back and held on. *Last time this woman did me a favor, I ended up coaching the cheerleading squad for the year.* Teaching girls how to shake their groove thang was definitely not her most developed talent.

Sister Joy glanced up from her desk and smiled. "Mr. Krupke! Please, sit." She motioned toward a chair in front of her metal desk.

He's here? Unable to stop herself, she turned to glance at him.

He gave the principle a friendly smile but hung back, standing about a foot away from Kate.

He sure is. She sighed.

Sister Joy cleared her throat, an obvious request for Kate's undivided attention.

But it wasn't easy for Kate to tear her gaze away, not with him standing that close. She tried once and failed. He was so much more pleasant to look at than Sister Joy, not that she had anything against older women.

He wasn't what most women would call traffic-stopping gorgeous, but in her book, he came darn close. If she had to label him, she'd call him bookish-handsome, with dark-framed glasses, slightly mussed hair that was a little long for a private high school teacher, and clothes that could probably fit a man almost twice his size—and he wasn't by any stretch of the imagination a small-framed man.

Since his first day, January fifth, exactly thirteen weeks and three days ago, she'd spent many a night trying to imagine what kind of body hid under those saggy pants and oversized sweaters.

He glanced her way, his dark brown eyes—the color of her favorite chocolate—settling upon hers for a moment.

Yes, handsome! Do you want to tell me something?

In response to her silent inquiry, he adjusted his tie and turned back to the principle. "You said you needed to speak with me?"

"Yes, Mr. Krupke. Ms. Evans and I were just discussing the Regional Music Educators' Conference this coming weekend."

"Yes." He adjusted his tie again.

"I wanted to send both of you this year, but my funds are limited. I know this is highly unusual, but I wanted to ask if you two could travel together to save a few pennies."

Travel together? Her face warmed. Had someone turned up the heat? Sister Joy was always so blasted cold.

As if she'd read Kate's mind, the principle buttoned her cable-knit cardigan sweater over her brown habit. "Now, I'm not asking you to share a room, or anything that atrocious. After all, we are a Catholic institution, and we must live by certain standards…"

Darn! What a shame.

"…I'd like you to simply ride together in a small, economy-minded vehicle."

Also known as my car. Kate felt herself smiling, even as a case of the nervous jitters overtook her body. Just imagining that bulk of a man crammed into the passenger seat of her subcompact made her tingly all over. He was so…large. And he'd be so…close. For hours.

About the author:

After penning numerous romances bordering on sweet, Tawny Taylor realized her tastes ran toward the steamier side of romance, and she wrote her first erotic romance, Tempting Fate, released March 2004. A second book, also a contemporary, titled Wet and Wilde, spotlighting a water phobic divorcee and a sexy selkie that no woman could resist, soon followed.

Tawny has been told she's sassy, brazen, and knows what she likes. So it comes as no surprise that the heroines in her novels would be just those kinds of women. And her heroes...well, they are inspired by the most unlikely men. Mischievous, playful, they know exactly how to push those fiery heroines' buttons.

Combining two strong-willed characters takes a certain finesse, something Tawny learned while studying psychology in college. And writing pages of dialogue dripping with sensual undertones and innuendo has also been a learned task, one Tawny has undertaken with gusto.

It is Tawny's fondest wish her readers enjoy each and every spicy, sex-peppered page!

Tawny Taylor welcomes mail from readers. You can write to her c/o Ellora's Cave Publishing at 1056 Home Avenue, Akron, Stow, OH 44310-3502.

Why an electronic book?

We live in the Information Age—an exciting time in the history of human civilization in which technology rules supreme and continues to progress in leaps and bounds every minute of every hour of every day. For a multitude of reasons, more and more avid literary fans are opting to purchase e-books instead of paperbacks. The question to those not yet initiated to the world of electronic reading is simply: *why?*

1. *Price.* An electronic title at Ellora's Cave Publishing and Cerridwen Press runs anywhere from 40-75% less than the cover price of the exact same title in paperback format. Why? Cold mathematics. It is less expensive to publish an e-book than it is to publish a paperback, so the savings are passed along to the consumer.
2. *Space.* Running out of room to house your paperback books? That is one worry you will never have with electronic novels. For a low one-time cost, you can purchase a handheld computer designed specifically for e-reading purposes. Many e-readers are larger than the average handheld, giving you plenty of screen room. Better yet, hundreds of titles can be stored within your new library—a single microchip. (Please note that Ellora's Cave and Cerridwen Press does not endorse any specific brands. You can check our website at www.ellorascave.com or

www.cerridwenpress.com for customer recommendations we make available to new consumers.)

3. *Mobility.* Because your new library now consists of only a microchip, your entire cache of books can be taken with you wherever you go.
4. *Personal preferences are accounted for.* Are the words you are currently reading too small? Too large? Too...**ANNOYING**? Paperback books cannot be modified according to personal preferences, but e-books can.
5. *Instant gratification.* Is it the middle of the night and all the bookstores are closed? Are you tired of waiting days—sometimes weeks—for online and offline bookstores to ship the novels you bought? Ellora's Cave Publishing sells instantaneous downloads 24 hours a day, 7 days a week, 365 days a year. Our e-book delivery system is 100% automated, meaning your order is filled as soon as you pay for it.

Those are a few of the top reasons why electronic novels are displacing paperbacks for many an avid reader. As always, Ellora's Cave and Cerridwen Press welcomes your questions and comments. We invite you to email us at service@ellorascave.com, service@cerridwenpress.com or write to us directly at: 1056 Home Ave. Akron OH 44310-3502.

ELLORA'S CAVE
ROMANTICA PUBLISHING

Printed in the United States
108240LV00006B/1/A